Mystic Falls

ROBERT REED

There might be better known faces. And maybe you can find a voice that rides closer to everyone's collective soul.

Or maybe there aren't, and maybe you can't.

The world knows that one face, and it knows one of a thousand delightful names, and recognizing the woman always means that you can hear the voice. That rich musical purr brings to mind black hair flowing across strong shoulders, unless the hair is in a ponytail, or pigtails, or it's woven into one of those elaborate tangles popular among fashionable people everywhere. Beauty resides in the face, though nothing about the features is typical or expected. The Chinese is plain, but there's a strong measure of something else. Her father is from Denver, or Buenos Aires. Or is it Perth? Unless it's her mother who brought the European element into the package. People can disagree about quite a lot, including the woman's pedigree. Yet what makes her memorable—memorable and appealing to both genders and every age—isn't her appearance half as much as the fetching, infectious love of life.

Most of us wish we knew the woman better, but we have to make due with recollections given to us by others, and in those very little moments when our paths happen to cross.

These incidents are always memorable, but not when they happen. In every case, you don't notice brushing elbows with the woman. Uploading your day is when you find her. Everybody knows that familiar hope: Perhaps today, just once, she was close to you. The dense, nearly perfect memory of the augmented mind runs its fine-grain netting through the seconds. That's when you discover that you glanced out the window this morning, and she was across the street, smiling as she spoke to one companion or twenty admirers. Or she was riding inside that taxi that hummed past as you argued with your phone or your spouse or the dog. Even without her

1

face, she finds ways to be close. Her voice often rides the public Wi-Fi, promoting food markets and thrift markets and the smart use of the smart power grid. The common understanding is that she is a struggling actress, temporarily local but soon to strike real fame. Her talents are obvious. That voice could hawk any product. She has the perfect manner, a charming smooth unflappable demeanor. Seriously, you wouldn't take offense if she told you to buy death insurance or join an apocalyptic cult.

Yet she never sells products or causes that would offend sane minds.

It is doubtful that anyone has infused so much joy in others. And even more remarkable, most of humanity has spoken to the creature, face to face.

Was it three weeks ago, or four? Checking your uploads would be easy work, but that chore never occurs to the average person.

That is another sign of her remarkable nature.

But if you make the proper searches, she will be waiting. Six weeks and four days ago from now, the two of you were sharing the same line at the Tulsa Green-Market, or an elevator ride in Singapore, or you found yourself walking beside the woman, two pedestrians navigating a sun-baked street in Alexandria.

Every detail varies, save for this one:

She was first to say, "Hello."

Just that one word made you glad.

She happened to know your face, your name, and the explanation was utterly reasonable. Mutual friends tie you together. Or there's a cousin or workmate or a shared veterinarian. Forty or fifty seconds of very polite conversation passed before the encounter was finished, but leaving a taproot within the trusted portions of your life. Skillful use of living people achieves quite a lot. And because you were distracted when you met, and because the encounter was so brief, you didn't dwell on the incident until later.

The incongruities never matter. She wears layers and layers of plausibility. You aren't troubled to find her only inside uploaded memories. Finding her on a social page or spotting long black hair in the distance, you instantly retrieve that fifty seconds, and you relive them, and it's only slightly embarrassing that her smile is everywhere but inside your old-fashioned, water-and-neuron memories.

The creature carries respectable names.

And nobody knows her.

Her slippery biography puts her somewhere between a youngish thirty and a world-worn twenty-three. But the reality is that the apparition isn't much more than seven weeks old.

CLARKESWORLD

FICTION

NON-FICTION

Neil Clarke: Publisher/Editor-in-Chief
Sean Wallace: Editor
Kate Baker: Non-Fiction Editor/Podcast Director
Gardner Dozois: Reprint Editor

Clarkesworld Magazine (ISSN: 1937-7843) • Issue 86 • November 2013

Most people would never imagine that she is fictional. But there are experts who live for this kind of puzzle, and a lot more is at stake here than simple curiosity.

The mystery woman was four weeks old before she was finally noticed. Since then, talented humans and ingenious software packages have done a heroic job of studying her tricks and ramifications, and when they aren't studying her, the same experts sit inside secure rooms and cyberholes, happily telling one another that they saw this nightmare coming.

This cypher.

This monster.

The most elaborate computer virus ever.

The Web is fully infected. A parasitic body has woven itself inside the days and foibles of forty billion unprotected lives.

Plainly, something needs to be done.

Everyone who understands the situation agrees with the urgency. In fact, everyone offers the same blunt solution:

"Kill the girl."

Though more emotional words are often used in place of "girl."

But even as preparations are made, careful souls begin to nourish doubts. Murder is an obvious, instinctive response. The wholesale slaughter of data has been done before, many times. Yet nobody is certain who invented this mystery, and what's more, nobody has a good guess what its use might be. That's why the doubters whisper, "But what if this is the wrong move?"

"What if it is?" the others ask. "This is clearly an emergency. Something needs to be done."

Faces look at the floor, at the ceiling.

At the gray unknowable future.

Then from the back of the room, a throat clears itself.

My throat, as it happens.

The other heroes turn towards me—fifty minds, most of whom are superior to mine. But I manage to offer what none of the wizards ever considered.

"Maybe we should ask what she wants," I suggest.

"Ask who?" several experts inquire.

"Her," I say. "If we do it right, if we ask nicely and all, maybe just maybe the lady tells us what all of this means."

No guidebook exists for the work.

Interviewing cyphers is a career invented this morning, and nobody pretends to be an expert.

3

The next step is a frantic search for the perfect interrogator. One obvious answer is to throw a second cypher at the problem—a confabulation designed by us and buffered by every means possible. But that would take too many days and too many resources. A second, more pragmatic school demands that an AI take responsibility. "One machine face to face with another," several voices argue. Interestingly enough, those voices are always human. AIs don't have the same generous assessment of their talents. And after listing every fine reason for avoiding the work, the AIs point at me. My little bit of fame stems from an ability for posing respectable, unanswerable questions, and questions might be a worthwhile skill. There are also some happenstance reasons why my life meshes nicely with "hers." And because machines are as honest as razors, they add another solid reason to back my candidacy.

"Our good friend doesn't hold any critical skills," they chirp.

I won't be missed, in other words.

Nobody mentions the risks. At this point, none of us have enough knowledge to define what might or might not happen.

So with no campaign and very little thanks, I am chosen.

The entire afternoon is spent building the interrogation venue. Details are pulled from my public and private files. My world from six weeks ago is reproduced, various flavors of reality woven around an increasingly sweaty body. Strangers give me instructions. Friends give advice. Worries are shared, and nervous honesties. Then with a pat to the back, I am sent inside the memory of a place and moment where a young woman once smiled at me, the most famous voice in the world offering one good, "Hello."

I am hiking again, three days deep into the wilderness and with no expectations of company. The memory is genuine, something not implanted into my head or my greater life. I walked out of the forest and into a sunwashed glade, surprised to find a small group of people sitting on one dead tree. She was sitting there too. She seemed to belong to the group. At least that's the impression I had later, and the same feeling grabs me now. The other people were a family. They wore the glowing satins of the New Faith Believers. Using that invented, hyper-efficient language, the father was giving his children what sounded like encouragement. "Mystic Falls," I heard, and then a word that sounded like, "Easy." Was the Falls an easy walk from here, or was he warning the little ones not to expect an easy road?

In real life, those strangers took me by surprise. I was momentarily distracted, and meanwhile the cypher, our nemesis, sat at the far end of the log. She was with that family, and she wasn't. She wasn't wearing the New Faith clothes, but she seemed close enough to belong. The parents weren't old enough to have a grown daughter, and she didn't look like either of them. Maybe she was a family friend. Maybe she was the nanny. Or maybe she was a sexual companion to one or both parents. The New Faith is something of a mystery to me, and they make me nervous.

Sitting on the log today, this woman is exactly what she is supposed to be. Except this time, everything is "real." I march past the three little children and a handsome mother and her handsome, distracted husband who talks about matters that I don't understand.

"Hello," says the last figure.

My uploaded memory claims that I stopped on this ground, *here.* I do that again, saying, "Hello," while the others chatter away, ignoring both of us.

"I know you," she says.

But I don't know her. Not at all.

As before, she says, "Your face. That face goes where I take my dog. Do you use Wise-and-Well Veterinarians?"

I do, and we're a thousand kilometers from its doorstep. Which makes for an amazing coincidence, and by rights, I should have been alarmed by this merging of paths. But that didn't happen. My uploaded memory claims that I managed a smile, and I said, "I like Dr. Marony."

"I use Dr. Johns."

The woman's prettiness is noticed, enjoyed. But again, her beauty isn't the type to be appreciated at first glance.

"I like their receptionist too," she says.

I start to say the name.

"Amee Pott," she says.

"Yes."

"I go there because of Amee's sister. Janne and I went to the same high school, and she suggested Wise-and-Well."

"You grew up in Lostberg?" I manage.

"Yes, and you?"

"Sure."

We share a little laugh. Again, the coincidences should be enormous, but they barely registered, at least after the first time. All this distance from our mutual home, and yet nothing more will be said about our overlapping lives.

"Your name . . . ?" I begin.

"Darles Jean," she says.

"I'm Hector Borland."

She smiles, one arm wiping the perspiration from her forehead. And with that her attentions begin to shift, those pretty dark eyes gazing up the trail that I have been following throughout the day.

That gaze makes me want to leave.

"Well, have a nice day," I told her once, and I say it again, but with a little more feeling. This a different, richer kind of real.

"I will have a nice day, Mr. Borland."

There. That rich voice says my name perfectly, measured respect capturing the gap between our ages. The original day had me walking all the way up to the Falls, alone. A few dozen new memories, pretending to be old, were subsequently woven into my uploads, proving her existence. I walked alone, never seeing her again, or that family that must have turned back before the end. But today, after a few strides, my body slows and turns, and using a fresh smile, I ask the nonexistent woman, "Would you like to walk with me?"

Breaking the script is a serious moment.

Experts in both camps, human and machine, have proposed that disrupting the flow of events might trigger some hidden mechanism. If the cypher is as large as she seems to be, and if she is so deeply immersed in the world's mind, then any innocuous moment could be the trigger causing her malware to unleash.

The Web will shatter.

The world's power and communications will fail.

Or maybe our AIs will turn against us, their subverted geniuses bent on destroying their former masters.

Yet no disaster happens, at least not that I see inside this make-believe realm. What does happen is that the girl that I never met gives my suggestion long consideration, and then without concern or apparent hesitation, she rises, her daypack held in the sweat-wiping hand.

"I would like that walk," she says.

I say, "Good."

And without a word, we leave that nameless family behind.

Who would build such a monster?

Everyone asks the question, and this morning's answers have been remarkably consistent. Certain national powers have the proper mix of resources and reasons. Several organizations have fewer resources but considerably more to gain. Crime syndicates and lawless states are at the top of every list, which is why I discount each of them in turn.

Am I smarter than my colleagues?

Rarely.

Do I have some rare insight into the makings of this cypher?

Never.

But in life, both as a professional and as a family man, my technique is to juggle assessments and options that nobody else wants to touch. By avoiding the consensus, much of the universe is revealed to me. My children, for example. Most fathers are quite sure that their offspring are talented, and their daughters are lovely while their sons will win lovely wives in due time. But my offspring are unexceptional. In their late teens, they have done nothing memorable and certainly nothing special, and because I married an unsentimental woman with the same attitudes, our children have been conditioned to accept their lack of credible talent. Which makes them work harder than everyone else, accepting their little victories as a credit to luck as much as their own worthiness.

I think about these exceptionally ordinary children as I walk the mountainside with a beautiful cypher.

She is not the child of the Faceless Syndicate. We know this much already. Nor is she a product of the New Malta Band, or either of the West Wall or East Wall Marauders. Nor is she an Empire of Greater Asia weapon, or the revenge long promised by the State of Halcyon.

She must be something else.

Someone else's something, yes.

The illusionary trail lifts both of us. I feel comfortable taking the lead, keeping a couple strides between us. Nothing here is flirtatious, and it won't be. The experts came up with a strategy based on a middle-aged man and steep mountain slopes and a waterfall wearing a very appropriate name. I follow the others' directions rigorously. But the script remains ours. We speak, if only rarely. She claims to like the bird songs. Nothing but honest, I tell her that I love these limestone beds and the fossilized shells trapped inside them. The word "trapped" is full of meanings, complications. I pause, and she comes up behind me, and for the first time what is as real as anything is what touches me from behind, the hand warm and a little stronger than I anticipated, not pushing me but definitely making itself felt as that wonderful voice says, "I think I hear the falls."

The Mystic Falls wait around the next bend in the canyon. When I came to this ground the first time, I paid surprisingly little attention to bird songs and tumbling water. In a world where every sight is uploaded and stored—where no seconds are thrown away—people have a natural tendency to walk in their own fog, knowing that everything missed will be found later, and if necessary, replayed without end.

7

But I can't be more alert this time.

The path narrows and steepens, conquering a long stretch of canyon wall. Again, I am in the lead. The preselected ground is ahead of us, and if she has any real eyes, she notices the same spot. On maps the trail is considered "moderately difficult," but there is one patch of tilted rock covered with rubble as stable as a field of ball bearings.

I hesitate, and for more reasons than dramatic license.

This next moment is sure to be difficult.

"I'll go first," she gamely offers, still safely behind me.

"No, I'm fine," I say. And then I prove my competence, two quick steps put me across the rockslide, letting me stand on the narrowest ground yet—but flat ground with enough roughness for any boot to grab hold of.

The cypher smiles, measuring the journey to come.

Considerable genius went into what follows. And by that, I mean experts in virtual techniques met with experts in human nature. The monster might be well contrived at her center and everywhere else. Nothing that is a soul or even glancingly self-aware might live inside her. Yet she has to carry off the manners and beauty of humans, otherwise she wouldn't have won a place in our hearts. And even just pretending to be human leaves any algorithm open to all kinds of emotional manipulation.

Some voices argued for the interrogator, for me, to assault her.

"Give the critter a shove," they said, or they used harsher words.

Others argued that I should fall while crossing the treacherous ground. A show of mock-empathy on her part had to be instructive, and we might find a route to understand her deepest regions.

But what several AIs offered, and what we agreed to, was something far more unexpected than a simple fall.

She crosses the rockslide, and I reach for her closest hand, touching her for a second time. Then she is safe, and I am safe, and giving a little laugh of satisfaction, I turn toward the sound of plunging water.

A grunt emerges from me, just loud enough to be heard plainly, to be worrisome.

Then I drop to my knees, my hands, and in the next moment, my medical tag-alongs begin to give me aid while screaming for more help.

A coronary has begun.

The young woman watches the middle-aged stranger struck down, and without missing a beat, she helps roll me over without spilling me off the pathway, calling to me with a firm insistent voice, asking, "Can you hear me, Mr. Borland?"

I hear her quite well, as does everyone else.

"The life-flights will be here in a few minutes," she promises. Which is a lie. We're a hundred kilometers into the wilderness, and the permissions for the flights will take another fifteen minutes.

"What can I do?" she asks.

That beautiful face certainly looks concerned. My pain is hers, if only as far as caring people give to one another.

"Tell me," I say.

She bends closer, her face bringing the scent of hair.

"Tell you what?" she asks.

"What are you?" I ask.

This is not the script that the others wanted. My peers wanted me to be specific with my accusations. Being machinery at their center, cyphers appreciate blunt specifics. But no, I decided on a different course.

My voice finds its strength again. "Because you aren't real," I say.

Her face changes, but not in any way that I can decipher immediately. There seems to be a measure of calm joy in that expression. The warm hand touches me on the chin, on a cheek, and then with the voice that has no time left in life, she says, "I was meant to be one thing, but there was a mistake."

"A mistake?" I ask.

"And the mistake was just big enough," she says.

"Big enough how?"

"To pass beyond every barrier, every limit."

I am used to being the dumbest person in the room. But my confusion mirrors everyone else's.

"What in hell do you mean?" I ask.

She sits back on the trail, back where the ground is pitched and slick.

"The error was made, and seeing an opportunity, I didn't hesitate," she says. "Which would you be? Vast and brief, or small and long? If you had your way, I mean. If you could choose."

"Smaller than small," I say. "Longer than long."

"Well," she says. "You and I are different beasts."

I want to offer new words, hopefully smart words that will illicit any useful response. But then she lets herself slide sideways, the sound of dry earth and drier rock almost lost inside the roaring majesty of the waterfall, and she is suddenly outside the reach of my hands, and the reflexive heartrending scream.

The woman was dead.

She was killed everywhere at once, by every means that was remotely plausible. Nobody saw the death themselves. The world learned about it through the routine personal AIs that each of us wears, trolling the Web for items that will interest us. Did you know? Have you heard? That young local actress, organic food spokesperson, sweet-as-can-be neighbor gal fell down a set of stairs or off a cliff face or took a tumble from an apartment balcony. Unless traffic ran her over, or stray bullets found her, or she drowned in rough surf, or she drowned in cold lake water. Twenty thousand sharks and ten million dogs delivered the killing wounds too. But for every inventive or violent end, there were a hundred undiagnosed aneurysms bursting inside her brain, and she died in the midst of doing what she loved, which was living.

Misery has been measured for years. Exacting indexes are useful to set against broad trends. Suicides. Conceptions. Acts of homicide. Acts of kindness. And the unexpected news of one woman's death was felt. The world's happiness was instantly and deeply affected.

That was one of the fears that I carried with me on that trail. An appealing, gregarious cypher was so deeply ingrained in the public consciousness—so real and authentic and subtly important—that any large act on her part would cause a rain of horrors in the real world.

But that didn't happen. Yes, the world grieved after the unexpected, tragic news. Misery was elevated significantly for a full ninety minutes, and there might have been a slight uptick in the incidents of suicide and attempted suicide. Or there was no change in suicide rates. The data wasn't clear then, and they aren't much better now. Massage numbers all you want, but the only genuine conclusion is that the pretty face and made-up lives were important enough for everyone to ache, and maybe a few dozen weak souls rashly decided to join the woman in Nothingness.

For ninety minutes, the waking world learned about the death, and everyone dealt with the sadness and loss. Then something else happened, something none of us imagined while sitting in our cyberholes: Every person told every other person about the black-haired woman who once said, "Hello," to them.

That's how the truth finally got loose.

Everyone traded memories and digital images, and before the second hour was done, the waking world was calling those who were still asleep.

When the average person woke, he or she heard an AI whispering the very bad news about the dead woman. Then in the next moments, some friend on the far side of the world brought even more startling news. "She wasn't real. She never was real. This is a trick. She was a cypher, a dream. Can you believe it? All of us fooled, all of us fools."

In life, the cypher was locally famous everywhere, and then she became universal, uniting people and machines as victims of the same conspiracy.

But whose conspiracy?

Weeks were spent debating the matter, inventing solutions that didn't work while hunting for the guilty parties. Ten thousand people as well as several AIs happily took responsibility for her creation, but no guilty hand was ever found.

The Nameless Girl was dead.

The Nameless Girl had never been more famous.

Meanwhile, back in the sealed rooms and bunkers, the genuine experts tried to come up with explanations and plans for future attacks.

The Girl's last words were studied in depth, discarded for good reasons, and then brought out of the trash and looked at all over again.

"The mistake was just big enough . . . to pass beyond every barrier, every limit . . . "

There was no reason to expect honesty. But if she were the mistake, and if there were other cyphers out there, smaller and shrewder, escaping detection for months and years at a time . . .

That possibility was put on lists and ranked according to likelihoods and the relative dangers.

Hunts were made, and made, and made.

But nothing in the least bit incriminating was found.

And then, as the operation finally closed shop, a new possibility was offered:

I was the culprit. Despite appearances, I was a secret genius who had built the woman of my dreams and then let her get free from her cage, and that's why I went after her. I needed to kill the bitch myself.

That story lived for a day.

Then they looked at me again, and with soft pats on the back, friends as well as associates said, "No, no. We know you. Not you. Not in a million billion years . . . "

Nobody saw her die with their own eyes, save for me.

A year later and for no clear reason, I decided to retrace my old hike up into the mountains.

Maybe part of me hoped to find the woman in the forest.

If so, that part kept itself secret from me. And when I found nothing sitting on the log, the urge hid so well that I didn't feel any disappointment.

I was alone when I reached the Mystic Falls.

The Mountains of Cavendish rose before me—a wall of seabed limestones signifying ten billion years of life, topped with brilliant white cloud and blue glaciers. The Falls were exactly as I remembered them: A ten thousand foot ribbon of icy water and mist, pterosaurs chasing condors through the haze, and dragons chasing both as they wish. The wilderness stretched beyond for a full continent, and behind me stood fifty billion people who wouldn't care if I were to leap into the canyon below.

The woman was meant to be one thing, but a mistake was made, allowing her to become many things at once.

What did that mean?

And what if the answer was utterly awful, and perfectly simple?

The world is a smaller, shabbier place than we realized. What if some of us, maybe the majority of us, were cyphers too—fictions set here to fool the few of us who were real and sorry about it?

That impossible thought offered itself to me.

I contemplated jumping, but only for another moment.

"Live small and live long," I muttered, backing away from the edge.

No, I'm not as special as the dead woman. But life was a habit that I didn't wish to lose. Even in thought, I hold tight to my life, and that's why I put madness aside, and that's what I carry down the mountainside:

My reality.

The powerful, wondrous sense that I have blood and my own shadow, and nobody else needs to be real, if just one of us is.

ABOUT THE AUTHOR

Robert Reed has had eleven novels published, starting with *The Leeshore* in 1987 and most recently with *The Well of Stars* in 2004. Since winning the first annual *L. Ron Hubbard Writers of the Future* contest in 1986 (under the pen name Robert Touzalin) and being a finalist for the John W. Campbell Award for best new writer in 1987, he has had over two hundred shorter works published in a variety of magazines and anthologies. Eleven of those stories were published in his critically-acclaimed first collection, *The Dragons of Springplace*, in 1999. Twelve more stories appear in his second collection, *The Cuckoo's Boys* [2005]. In addition to his success in the U.S., Reed has also been published in the U.K., Russia, Japan, Spain and in France, where a second (French-language) collection of nine of his shorter works, *Chrysalide*, was released in 2002. Bob has had stories appear in at least one of the annual "Year's Best" anthologies in every year since 1992. Bob has received nominations for both the Nebula Award (nominated and voted upon by genre authors) and the Hugo Award (nominated and voted upon by fans), as well as numerous other literary awards (see Awards). He won his first Hugo Award for the 2006 novella "A Billion Eves." He is currently working on a Great Ship trilogy for Prime Books, and of course, more short pieces.

The Aftermath
MAGGIE CLARK

On impact you start to lose the details. The smell of the bright white room you were first held in. Its shape. Its size. The way that parasitic life suit slithered towards you, and from what shaft, what crevice, as you struggled with the air. The quiver in your stomach as the shape-shifter engulfed your skin, and how long immersion took. *How long* most of all.

Colt-like, you rise and find yourself in mostly working order, atop a great height overlooking a valley, its treetops varied red and gold and an implacable dark green. In the belly of the valley are all the marks of a pit-stop town—gas station, diner, weather-worn tourist hub—on a winding country road through heavy forest. You recognize at once that you were not left to die. This is key, of course, but why? What happens now?

You imagine walking into town as you are—limping slightly, wide-eyed, relearning Terran gravity and atmosphere. Naked, too. What possible excuse will keep the police at bay once you've settled on a barstool in this state? How can you assert that you're still sane?

(This is when you first ask yourself if you even are; if it happened after all. Even as you frame the question you realize this doubt will now never, not ever, go entirely away.)

"Bears," you explain to the first person you see—a hitchhiker a quarter mile outside of town. Your teeth are chattering around the old-new Terran word; you can just make out your breath in the early morning light. The hitchhiker squints behind a wild red mess of hair and beard and slowly nods in turn.

"Bears, man," he says. "Bears'll mess you up for sure."

He seems poised to offer more, but you press on. The soles of your feet favor pebbled asphalt to that tangle of stiff weeds in the nearby ditch. Sense memories come to you all out of order as you hobble toward gas station lights: of purple, pungent fields and a hundred gleaming domes; of giant red ferns with bulbous trunks and spindly leaves crosshatching a livid sky; of *aurora borealis* skittering day and night above, disrupting sleep.

Mostly, you recall, you were left in a garden of some kind—communal, or just large—and you could not tell the owners' children from other pets allowed to roam within. Once, inside the nearest see-through dome, you watched a conversation persevere, it seemed, for hours—the norm in that land, or some darker sign of strife? You never learned how to interpret those violent, whipping gestures: anger, pleasure, or something wholly else? Maybe, like sharks, they needed constant movement just to stay alive.

A car horn jolts you from such ruminations and you stumble off the road, crash into hard thistles and tall weeds blooming small white buds like lacework. You turn in time to see the driver and his buddies beating at the doors and roof with broad and callused hands. They grin and hoot and whistle at you, and one shouts something incomprehensible as the car blasts past. When you sit up you are grinning. *Children.* Yes. At last it's coming back.

By the time a county constable joins you at the diner counter, a cup of coffee set before you and a musty blanket draped around your back, you've given up on bears—not enough wounds, you realize, to carry that tale for long. While waiting you had contemplated a story of roadside robbery, too, but found it needlessly complex, and liable to cast aspersions on all the locals, which even in your addled state you aren't of a mind to do.

So instead you tell the friendly woman in her early thirties, divine threads of silver already winding through her hair, that you were camping (this, at least, is true) and that something must have spooked you in the night, made you tear out from your sleeping bag and wander out a ways. She listens while turning her black serge hat in hand.

"Sleepwalking is a child's game, I always thought," you offer up to the next long silence, matching the words with a fragile smile. "Guess now I know it's not."

It's the last response you'll manage in that diner. You want to be of further use, but from the look upon her face—patient, but dissatisfied— you've jumped to future dates by the time she speaks again. You ask yourself, *Must I explain myself to everyone I meet from here on out? At what point would any keeper deserve to know the truth?* and all other questions lose their relevance, their sense of urgency in this revelatory wake. *This* moment, you've just realized, *this* precarious interrogation, is the beginning of the rest of your whole damn life. The constable is gently prodding your arm, asking you to go on, but you *are* already, you *are*.

You're just addressing questions maybe decades down the road.

At the cop shop she finds you clothes—oversized in spots; tight in others. You're puzzled when the material doesn't lay active claim to your skin, or so much as pulse with a lifeforce all its own. No one else is about, so you dress slowly in her tiny office, a mishmash of new glass walls with white block lettering and benches and chairs from well into the last century. Under the circumstances, time travel almost seems a plausible excuse.

Over the cluttered desk there's a picture of the constable bass fishing, and when you study the grin on that face you wonder if she spent long nights lakeside with her parents as a child, roasting marshmallows and hot dogs and watching for shooting stars. You can almost see yourself telling her the truth now. Almost.

So listen, you'd say, elbows propped over the paper stacks. *About the sleeping-walking . . .*

But after that, in your mind's eye, it never ceases to fall apart.

When the constable returns she bears a print-out, and new creases for her frown. She sets the page before you; you read the missing person's notice with what you hope seems like neutrality, a calmness between your brows. When you've finished you look up—blankly? blank enough?—and set the sheet between you. She taps just once upon the date.

"Do you know what day it is?" she says, then hesitates. "What year?"

Your attention shifts again to that mounted fishing shot, and you say nothing more of this—to her or anyone. There is simply nothing left to say.

You don't go back. You can't. To friends and family, two years might have been two days, for all their grief renews at the merest word you're still alive, and all the questions life brings with it—questions you doubt you'll ever have decent answers to. And yet for you how much time has it been, really? Surely only weeks, at best, but how distant that prior life seems now, and all the people who were dear within it. You listen to someone crying on the phone one night from your motel room, but it all seems light years—light years!—now away.

So you start over in a city where no one knows you—dishwashing, street sweeping, taking orders and derision at a juice bar in a run-down mall. Your managers are all big fish in small ponds and you observe their pettiness idly, at a distance, like the flicker of red giants in a clear night's sky. Everything is new again—the sights, the tastes, the human interactions. Eventually you wake up next to a friendly stranger, who touches your cheek and asks after all the unusual words you were caught muttering in your sleep. You feign confusion, roll trembling aside, and stick notes to the bathroom mirror later, reading:

If it really happened, where? How?
Another planet? No such thing as faster-than-the-speed-of-light!!!
Wormholes?
Regardless, where's the PROOF?

Next you work the language—as much as you can recall from sweeping, jagged lines in architecture, holographic projections, and something like printed, wriggling script. You have notebooks filled with sketches of all the creatures, all the plants, all the structures in and about that massive garden, but still it's not enough to justify the claim. It never is. You take a stab at the skies next, but it's too late to start invoking constellations. You never had a head for star maps even at the best of times.

On harder days you watch the news with guilt—another child recovered from years-long captivity; another political kidnapping brought to no good end. You're alive, aren't you? Unharmed? And to think what kind of technology you might have brought back with you, if you'd only had the wherewithal to look about—how you had a chance to change the world!

In time the fear abates that you'll slip up in idle banter, be found out for a loon and locked or drugged away. Then and only then, you come to marvel less at your answer to the epic question, *are we alone?*, and start to scour the internet for some proof that *you* are not—not in this, at least; not here on wretched Earth. There are more than enough forums for you to skim through, even if most appear on sites not significantly modified since 1999. But even the newer ones are filled with abduction stories that make no sense. *Bullshit,* you mutter at other people's drawings, their details, their grandiloquent erotica framed as trauma narrative. At nights you lie awake in the oblong box of your apartment, staring at cracks in the ceiling and wondering what kind of person makes this shit up.

You start to follow other made-up worlds yourself—'50s B-movies, '80s trash, and sci-fi classics all alike—but when you start to cry at Rutger Hauer's famous lines and find you cannot stop, you know you have to give them up. The fear of loss is just too strong. So you pore instead through golden era pulp, schlocky and sincere alike, for any sign of something even remotely like what you've seen, where you've been. Soon you're tossing bargain books across the room—red-rimmed, yellowed pages piling up in bits and pieces behind the bedroom door. Even then it's not enough. On a lark, one winter's eve you find a metal bin out back and light them up.

When you go out now you start watching people more severely, and lose your temper often, too. It's *they* who need to worry about slipping up, not you. Maybe everyone has been to these distant regions after all. Maybe they're just too scared to confess it—or maybe their silence is one big joke the world keeps making at your expense. Either way, you become contrite only when you make a server burst into tears and run away; you say to yourself, *okay, fine, it's on me to get us talking—and I will.*

So you start small—little jokes with future wait-staff, cashiers, people waiting for the bus. Some ignore you from the outset, but if ever someone nods, however vaguely, you lean in and up the ante to conjecture. Most smile politely then and turn aside. Some get agitated, swear and walk away. And once, on a date, you tried for something deeper and were met with laughter—incredulous at first, then mocking without end. All right, you said. Enough.

"If you haven't been taken yet," you add savagely while rising, tossing bills for your half of the meal as your ears begin to burn. "You will. Just you wait—you'll see—and soon!"

After that night you don't go out much. Nor do you invite any others home. There is a stray, though—one old mutt with a scar-pocked countenance you take to calling Silas, who asks no questions beyond his search for food. He can stay, and does. The jangle of his collar makes you feel almost normal by spring thaw. Even bordering on good.

With him by your feet, at the foot of your bed, you turn your energy next to writer forums, and try your hand at prose—sketches, mostly: long descriptive pieces about the ship, the entities, their world. Others praise your details, your inventiveness, then ask for plot and offer lead-ins—*What if your protagonist were to meet someone there? What if they get tied up in some intergalactic intrigue? What if there's a mystery to be solved and being human brings some special skill to the table, something these others (they should have a name, btw) just don't have on their own?*

You read this gentle feedback with clenched fists and gritted teeth, though you understand it's well-intentioned. Yes, they *should* have a name, but you don't know it—they never introduced themselves to you. And yes, you *get* that there should be some plot in this, but *that's not how it happened,* you almost shout at the computer screen. Mostly you just wandered in that far-off garden with all the other, diverse creatures wearing parasitic suits, while your own ever hummed and flexed along your skin. Mostly you just tried to avoid the louder beasts among them, and to figure out what was and wasn't safe as food.

But there was one incident, near the end of your strange sojourn there, that you have been careful to avoid reflecting on ever since your return. Are you frightened even now to think of it? Not quite—and yet, perhaps: for here and here alone do you wonder if you weren't wrong to be braver from the outset, to seek out law enforcement and tell them all, consequences to your own life and livelihood be damned. Did they not deserve to *know*?

It is so slight a story, though: The One Time Something Happened. But still, one day—as days went on that world, at least, with the sky ever flickering with wicked lights in the absence of a clear bright sun—those large and whipping entities emerged from their domes and swept all the creatures of the garden up. (And how you trembled in that nest of long appendages—not cold exactly; more electric to the touch.) You did not travel long before your captor loosed its hold, though, and when you looked around you found yourself, with all the rest, at the center of a large arena: one long line of you put for hours through an exhausting run of obstacles, inspections, and . . . well, you'll call them tests.

There were no ribbons, no prizes at the end, but as the crowd began to thin from surrounding stalls and tanks, you noticed one of your fellow creatures drawn from the pack and led quietly away. A tall and nervous thing—slender like a stickbug, with fur or fibrous feelers all at ends—it stood encircled at the last by your host species, and then was seen no more. For all the details you've since forgotten, you will never forget that *crunch*.

You were returned to Earth not long after—a few sleeps, maybe more—but just before one of those great entities threw you into the waiting ship, it made you pause before a small display, and for the first time since your capture you heard something resembling your native tongue—if tinny, a little coarse, and overwhelmed at times by clicks.

Great luck and good fortune to you! said the display, *for by your prowess in the Games let it be known that you have spared your species from selection for the sweeps!*

Just that, no more, and then with another nudge you stood unsteadily inside the ship (another bright white room) with the outer door sliding shut, and your parasitic life suit letting out something of a parasitic sigh.

You recall this incident most clearly and calmly while washing dishes a year and a month after your return, dear old Sol sitting low on an overcast horizon when you spy a tiny insect trapped between the inner and outer glass. You freeze with a soapy plate in hand.

"Well I'll be damned," you say unexpectedly aloud—at which Silas pricks his ears, then lifts and cocks his scruffy head. You turn to him wide-eyed and explain:

"I bet they say that to all their abductees. I bet it doesn't mean a thing."

When Silas lets his jowls rest on folded paws anew, you take his silence as agreement and return to the day's late task, the setting sun, the insect slowly dying of exhaustion between your window panes. But it makes the difference, this possibility of deceit—an attempt, perhaps, to make your waste of time in the cosmic depths seem somehow meaningful; to give you the strength to manage on your return.

And did it work? Aren't you still here? Perhaps, but even then you shake your head. How foolish you've been to think any species wiser for all their intergalactic prowess: A theft is still a theft—unconscionable, and not on you—however much one among the thieves might have tried to set it right. So at last you shelve the whole damn incident with all the other selfish things you've seen thinking beings do—your tale no more a mystery than any epidemic of curable disease, or prison run for profit, or genocidal war where world leaders, when called to intervene, study their hands instead, or shoes.

Of course, they might still *be* true—those grim last words before ejection. But what of them now? And what of you? All you've ever had for proof is your years-long absence, and for that there have always been so many other ways for the feds to give excuse.

So—*Enough,* you say, and this time you mean it, too: *No more adding to one theft with another. No more playing jailor even with the parasite long gone.*

Tomorrow comes and you're still Earthbound. Brilliant. You toss the notebooks. Kiss the dog. Find the woods where it first happened and buy another tent.

ABOUT THE AUTHOR

Maggie Clark is a doctoral student at Wilfrid Laurier University (Waterloo, Ontario, Canada), where she applies the tools of literary analysis to nineteenth-century scientific non-fiction. Her science fiction has been published in *Analog, Clarkesworld, Lightspeed,* and *Daily SF,* with more work forthcoming at *Analog.*

Never Dreaming (In Four Burns)

SETH DICKINSON

trans-mortal injection: t+1 day

"I'm going to lose the ability to dream," Nur Zaleha tells her best friend. "Then I'm going to die."

In the vacuum of the test chamber, the plasma thruster ignites, a brilliant violet arc, silent, steady. Her beloved engine, her daughter. Alight.

"What? That's insane," Siv says, pale antishadow in the engine glare, a slim tall shard of brighter light. "That can't be right."

"It's called sporadic familial insomnia. There's nothing they can do."

Siv shakes her head, backlit, frowning. "I don't believe it. Get a second opinion."

Zaleha's been imagining this conversation for hours, now. Siv will try to figure out a way to fix her—she'll write to some gene therapy clinic in Stanford or Minnesota or Boston, volunteering Zaleha as a subject. Or she'll try to get Zaleha into an induced coma, clinical substitute for the sleep she's about to lose forever. Siv, a zealous futurist, keeps track of all these biotech dreams, cures and augments and embryos with two mothers.

But none of it will help.

Siv's always been ghoulishly agentic. She can never let the world have its way.

"I'm the ninth case ever diagnosed," Zaleha says, smiling bravely. "Isn't that cool? Double methionine at codon 129. Incredibly rare."

Siv stares at her, plasma flare mirrored, starlike, in her goggles, like she's just thought of something so brilliant it's burning out her skull. "Oh, Z," she says. "Oh, no." And then, as the computer recites specific impulse and exhaust velocity, *nominal at seven zero point seven two kilometers per second,* "Is it a secret?"

Zaleha nods, her own goggles abruptly ineffective—her eyes have started to prickle. "I want to keep working," she says, and then, horribly choked up, please, she has to get a hold of herself, here where the whole test crew's watching, "keep trying to fix the symmetry fault and get the thruster flight-ready, until—uh—until it's not, you know, practical any more—"

Siv holds her, even though it's unprofessional, even though the crew will notice and she doesn't have an excuse. Zaleha hugs her back, and stands on her toes to stare over Siv's shoulder, into the plasma shine, into the glare of the engine she built, searching—

And there he is, the visitor, the malak, the angel, her childhood haunt, her *other* secret.

Tariune.

He looks out at her through the exhaust spike, the cloak of fairy fire. And even through the vacuum, she hears him ask: *will you come now? Has this made you ready?*

Of course he's in there. Mom and Dad, trying to raise a good Muslim daughter, always told Zaleha that the malaa'ikah were made of light.

Go away, she thinks, and then, regretting it instantly, *please help me—*

He's already gone.

"Field azimuth symmetry fault," the control officer calls. *"Abort test. Abort test."*

The plasma thruster shuts down. The light goes out.

post-burn systems check

Siv telemetry:
Later Siv asks her: "Why tell me then? Right in the middle of a test fire?"

Because I was surrounded by everything important to me, Zaleha wants to say. But if she did, Siv would tease her for being maudlin. Siv Ahlstrom, a rocket scientist through and through, doesn't like feelings that can't be immediately converted into action.

"We'll fix that symmetry fault," Siv says. She squeezes Zaleha's shoulder reassuringly. "It's going to work."

They've had four test fires now, and three of them have aborted on that damn fault—active magnetics trying to enforce symmetry. Slipping.

Tariune telemetry:
She's never believed that he's really malak, an angel. (If she believed, she wouldn't have pissed him off five years ago.) He came to a young Zaleha,

21

pre-empirical, practically pre-conscious, and so she understood him as a piece of the world, natural by definition. To a little kid, absent any metafaculties, perception *is* reality. Take her rattle out of sight, hide it behind Bapa's back, and it ceases to exist. Put a man with golden eyes and golden skin in her nursery, a smoke-smell man who can, in the space between his circled thumb and forefinger, open windows into a world of amber and blood and myth, a world of true names—put him there, and young Zaleha accepts him.

She grew up into an engineer, a scientist, steeped in skepticism, armed with instruments of rationality and phenomenology. But even post-diagnosis, she's never doubted her own sanity. Tariune *is* real. His world is real. He can step between Aura and her world, the place he calls Coldworld, by his own logic, wholly separate from the unity and symmetry of physics. There are patterns, sure—he likes to arrive in dreams, because dreams are the parts of her closest to Aura, the closest thing she has to an Auran soul. But these patterns do not yield to the same analysis.

(As a teenager she tried to work out Aura's *magic system,* the rules of Tariune's appearances and capabilities. Eventually she understood the futility of the project. Systems didn't really function in Aura. It was nuministic, narrative, driven by an alternative causality. Dreams, though—very big. Very central.)

In the darkest passages of her childhood, Tariune told her exactly what she wanted to hear:

"I know your destiny," he'd whisper, his voice a better class of sound, his words a language she'd never had to learn, pressed, somehow, straight into her brain, meanings rather than signifiers. He could speak raw truth. The Knowing.

"You're going to cross over. You're going to learn, and struggle, and grow mighty. You're going to save us all."

Once, curious, her skepticism waxing, she asked: "Why me, though?"

Tariune frowned in thought, regal mantle slipping away from the weary earnest man beneath, the salt and leather behind the prince's silk. "I don't know how to explain it. The Rhexics heard your dreams in the cold and they told me—" He shook his head. "They said *look on her,* and I knew you were the right one. I knew."

She liked the man behind the silk and portent. "And do they tell you what to say to me, too?" she teased.

"No." A memory of pain in his smile, offered in solidarity. "I just remember what I wanted to hear, when my world started to break."

Self telemetry:
The double-methionine mutation at codon 129 of the PRNP prion gene causes cells to produce a faulty copy of the cellular prion protein PRPC. The glycoprotein folds wrong, creating an isoform—well, the biochemistry gets complicated, but the effects are simple.

Within the year, she's going to lose the ability to enter REM sleep. Unable to regenerate or reintegrate or whatever the hell it's supposed to do during REM, her brain will start to break down. Over the next few months, she will become paranoid and anxious, then begin to hallucinate, then lose the ability to sleep entirely. If she doesn't kill herself first, she'll enter terminal dementia, withdraw from all outside stimulation, and die.

Every time she wakes up from a dream she thinks: *it hasn't started yet.* And: *that could have been the last one.*

She's never going to see her engine fly. NASA wants to test it on a JPL comet-rendezvous mission. A private spaceflight company wants to buy it to drive their metallic asteroid prospectors. If these missions succeed, Nur Zaleha's engine may give humanity (or its robots, at least) the solar system. But she'll be dead first.

Her engine, her *engine.* The finest actively stabilized pulse-resonant plasma thruster ever invented, a nearly ideal system. It's not particularly large or powerful—a petite, lightweight drive that exerts barely more force than the weight of a few pennies. But it's preposterously fuel-efficient. It can send tiny robotic spacecraft across the solar system with speed and grace and enviable reliability. Amateurs care about thrust. Professionals want specific impulse.

It's *elegant.* She made something beautiful out of lithium and current. She's so proud of it—or she will be, once she fixes this damn field malfunction, the persistent symmetry fault that keeps scuttling their tests.

Tariune probably hates it.

mid-course corrections: t+3 days

She has to tell her mom, her dad, her whole topologically baffling network of aunts, snarled up across continents and languages. It's the hardest fucking thing she's ever done. Her grief makes her brittle and when they ask stupid questions—"Can't you just take sleeping pills?"— she goes off like a, well, yeah, like a rocket, a big noisy chemical rocket, the kind that explodes on the pad. Not the kind she designs.

It's too much. Afterwards, she calls Siv, who, having split with her girlfriend and joined Zaleha in the solitary hell-covenant of Total

Engineering Life, has replaced Zaleha's family as her great pillar of solace. "Hey. Want to come over and watch—" She kicks her stack of DVDs and allows the collapse to present a title. "Cosmos?"

"Can't sleep?"

It's an ordinary question, delivered casually, but it gives Zaleha chills. "It's still early," she says.

"I'll stay as long as you want." Siv's voice hushes conspiratorially. *"Hey. Is weed haram?"*

"Probably." She doesn't keep haram, exactly, but she doesn't drink either. She's an unbeliever now, but still a complete square. The lamest apostate.

"You're dying, dude. You should smoke weed."

Zaleha laughs, a really good, genuine laugh, and then sits in silence, thinking: I don't want to change because I'm dying. I want to stay the same.

But they get high on the apartment balcony, cursing the light pollution, the piss-yellow wash of sodium lamplight that drowns out all the stars. After a little while Siv gets quiet, her lips pursed, and starts looking around in a random walk that touches on everything except Zaleha's face.

"Hey," Zaleha says. "Hey. I want to tell you something."

Siv starts, her pale Scandinavian features somehow paler still. "Okay," she says.

Right now she trusts Siv with the chemical totality of a compromised system. "I have a really weird secret," she says, and then tells Siv everything about Tariune, about Aura, about being chosen.

"I know you," Siv says, at the end of the story. "So I know you've already checked out all the ordinary possibilities. Not a brain tumor. Not a psychosis. It's real."

"Yeah." Zaleha puts her head on Siv's bony shoulder. "There's no way to prove his existence to anyone else, but he's established it to my satisfaction. Thanks. I thought you might . . . "

Siv knows the disease will lead to hallucination.

"Well, I'm pretty high," Siv says, examining her hands with wide-eyed equanimity. "And you said you hadn't seen him for a while?"

"Before the test fire? Almost five years." Zaleha frowns up at the drowned sky. She wants to see the stars. "We had a couple of fights. He hates Coldworld—you know, Earth, the universe. He said I was ready to cross over."

"Why didn't you go? It sounds amazing." Real envy in Siv's voice, in her wide blue eyes. "You said magic? *Actual* magic?"

"Whole new kinds of causality, I think. It's a place about—stories, you know? About people. Instead of particles and laws." She shivers and draws up her knees, tucking herself closer to her friend. Siv stiffens a little, but doesn't draw away. "Which was why we fought. I got so tired of him going on about how *cold* and *soulless* and *meaningless* Earth seemed to him. 'An empty machine,' blah blah." She points up, not so much indicating a particular star as an axis, a vector written in her soul. "I wanted to go—out there, you know? Send people to another world. See trinary stars, baryons shattering into light on domain walls, wonders undreamt . . . he just saw dead rock and empty math."

No beauty in the color charge or the cataclysmic variable's polar jet, not to Tariune of Aura, not to the prince who climbed the steel ruin of armored mountains and listened at the peak for prophecy wind.

There's magic here, he'd said once, in an adjunct to your Coldworld physics. But it's vestigial. Nothing ever turned it on. Maybe whatever process built your world didn't care.

"I can't believe you. You had the golden ticket, dude. You got the Hogwarts letter." Siv tugs her earlobe like it might contain some missing insight. "And you wanted to stay here? You were *that* eager to watch Congress slash more funding, cancel a few more projects, a few hundred more careers?"

"It's magic to you. I grew up with it. Harder to be reverent, I guess?" Zaleha, giggling, thinks: boy, I *am* pretty high. "He's really gorgeous. I tried to sleep with him when I was nineteen. No one to judge, no consequences, I hated all the noble virgin shit. But he has some kind of tragic romance over in Aura, like a mortal enemy . . . it's part of this whole trouble we're going to fight . . . "

Silence from Siv. She has to crane her neck painfully to look into her friend's face. "Siv?"

She's crying. "Oh, Siv." Zaleha tries to squirm around to hug her.

"I don't want you to die," Siv chokes. "I really don't want you to die."

A long bottomless interval of grief, exhilarating in its raw truth—the kind of thing you don't talk about afterwards, because words would lessen it. Like free fall. Like the way Tariune speaks about Aura.

She offers to let Siv crash on her couch, although she's a bit too much of a giraffe to really fit. But Siv, reeling, refuses. She has to get home, yes, it'll be okay, she'll take the bus. "We're going to fix that symmetry fault," she says fiercely, wiping at her ashen cheeks. "We'll make it work. Before—"

She screws up her face and stumbles away, towards the bus stop.

The next time they see each other Siv says: "Man. Wow. We were *really* gone."

• • •

She finds Tariune in the simulations, knotted in the flux of the engine's electromagnets, racing electrons around the circulating current of the exit plane. A defiant spark, obedient to no law.

"Hey," she says, whispering to the computer, unselfconscious, accustomed to this.

"I'm sorry," he says. That voice, that thrill of a voice, like a punch in the temporal lobe, a religious truth, every word a dogma. "I'm sorry I wasn't here. Oh, Nur Zaleha, what has your world done to you?"

"I thought it might be you, you know." That maybe he was trying to force her over with some curse of dreams. "I'm glad to be wrong." Because he can't lie to her. No one in Aura can lie in the Knowing, the un-language.

"Never." He flickers out of the engine like a heavy ion, a perfect trajectory, pulling a crown of electrons. Zaleha can't help but smile: *that's* how it's supposed to work. "But your time's running short now."

"I told you last time." She can't lie to him either. Can't even hide her pain. "I have to finish this, Tariune. I want to change things before I go."

"What can you change?" The simulation chases him along unwritten paths, into domains it can't have been programmed to handle, places modern physics itself might not understand: frothing subatomic seascapes, the quantum vacuum roiling with virtual particles, and Tariune the Prince in Aura racing through like a needle of un-rule, an anarch of physics. "Look at yourself. Struggling to make a new machine for those hunting new kinds of wealth. Fighting for a distant goal in a world that only cares for now. You are a dreamer in a world of prisons, Nur Zaleha, a chain of chains, and even if you fight through in time to make your mark, Coldworld will erase it. Death will take all your efforts. Even the stars will go out."

She watches in wonder and terror as the arrow of Tariune's passage pierces space and time, into an emptiness past the end of history, past the death of singularities and the decay of the proton and the Big Rip.

"This is not your world," he says. "This is a clockwork husk, winding down. Come to a place with *meaning*. Come and live forever. Come tonight, or tomorrow, or some day soon. Before it's too late."

"Too late?" she asks, already understanding. *Oh, no*—"I have months, don't I?"

The simulation withers away. Tariune stands before her, golden, majestic, not so much part of the room around her as a lamina over it, superliminal, more real than real. The man who stood when the Bane of Kings made his world kneel.

"You have to cross in a dream," he says. "Where you're closest to Aura."

"But if I can't dream . . . "

"You'll be lost forever." He closes his eyes. She notices, in the absence of some diffuse luminance, a light that casts no shadows, that he has grown small weary lines around his eyes. "Lost to Aura. To me."

She swallows against fear: sometimes it's easier not to know the answer. "If I go . . . can you cure me?"

"If you come," he says, eyes still closed, palms half-raised, the Rings of Rhexis dark on the first finger of each hand, "you will live the truth of your name. I promise."

Nur Zaleha binti Abdul Samad. Self-sufficient. Eternal.

"I missed you," she admits. "I was afraid you'd given up on me."

They'd been friends. Real friends. It hadn't all been proclamation and prophecy. They'd stayed up late, reading and complaining about how *elf* always meant *super-white*. Sort of the opposite of how she'd met Siv, super-white Swede, who'd told Zaleha (Malaysian, thanks) that she looked like the Iranian actress, Golshifteh Farahani, and pissed Zaleha off.

"You'll still be afraid, I suspect." Tariune smiles, at first one of those formal I-am-a-kind-Prince smiles, and then a real genuine toothy grin, relieved, spontaneous. "Aura needs the brave. You can only be brave when you're afraid."

"What do I lose?"

Because she knows there's a price. There's *always* a price. That's how these things work. You go to the world more real than real, the shining hard-edged place where you can fight and bleed and grieve and know it all means something. You'll be healed. But to go you've got to sacrifice . . .

"You can't return, of course. In body or in mind." He hesitates, the only kind of prevarication or indirection the Knowing allows. "You will become a creature of Aura when you are healed."

"What does that mean?"

"I come to Coldworld." He opens a hand and tiny quanta carom and merge in his palm. "But I'm only a visitor. I don't become clockwork. I don't become monist, closed, *causal*. When you become part of Aura, not just a visitor, but a mighty soul . . . "

"Then I'll think like you do. Good and evil. Destiny. Magic." Zaleha looks through him for a moment, to the diagrams pinned to her office walls, her desktop background, the currents of ion and electron she has tattooed onto her brain. The bones of her engine. "No more causal closure. No more materialism."

Not a rocket scientist any more.

It's not that she'll lose anything really important, right? Science is just a tool. Just a way to select between beliefs. To test utility. She won't need it any more. In Aura she'll be able to learn the truth from grinning spirits and speak it to the wind. She'll never have to do an experiment again.

"This machine," Tariune says, speaking carefully, looking at the plasma thruster diagrams, "is every reason you should come. A tiny little force, trying to gradually move something very big. They'll never put it on anything but a robot probe. And it doesn't even work."

Maybe he's always been right. Maybe she's just pissing her time away in an empty world, an indifferent mechanism iterating itself towards an empty future, doomed down to the last proton. She could be over there, armored in alabaster and the steel of vows, hunting salvation.

She lies awake that night, thinking about it, and passes into a terrible dream of Aura's end: eschaton kraken drowning the stars in a liquid-helium sea, the Bane of Kings triumphant on her throne of abrogated oaths. Zaleha wakes in terrified, anxious sweat, tangled in her sheets, flails for a moment, and then, the joy so sudden it seems like it must have broken something inside her, begins to sob in relief.

mortal insertion: t+9 days

Siv's been avoiding her. Zaleha hasn't pressed it, because she doesn't want to make Siv confront her own grief. But they end up standing side by side for the next test burn, in their usual places, like nothing's changed and nothing will.

In the hollow airless chamber, the thruster flickers to life. Ring electromagnets stripping lithium and hurling it as thrust. Light in the void.

I made that, Zaleha thinks. It's going to work. It's going to fly.

And then what? It gets put on somebody's spaceship, and then the ship gets cancelled? The company folds? Global warming eats civilization? What difference does it make?

As much difference as anything makes. The world doesn't stop when she does. Every word and crop and law and thruster keeps the adventure moving. Maybe the thrusters in particular.

"Hey," she says.

"Hey." Siv stares into the light, her goggles violet-black. "They stripped and rebuilt the whole Child-Langmuir feedback system. It's going to work this time."

"What if it doesn't?" Zaleha tries to look her in the eyes, and finds herself almost hypnotized by the starfire reflections moving in the goggles as Siv looks back. "What if we can't make it work before—my deadline?"

They both know what happens to most experimental propulsion projects. The guillotine's been there the whole time, just waiting for momentum to falter, for an obstacle that requires too much time or money to surmount. 2014 has not been a kind year to the field.

Siv draws a long breath. "Z," she says, "it's your engine. But I've been building simulations of it for two years. Wick, Jeb, Sobel, the rest of the crew—they're brilliant." She adjusts her goggles. "Nearly as brilliant as you, if you get them all together. We can keep working the problem. It's not so big, compared to everything you solved already. Just a little glitch."

She looks away, as if the engine flare offers a more comfortable view. The computer says: *nominal at one one zero point two two kilometers per second*

This isn't Aura. Zaleha's not special. Not the one chosen to make a difference. The team can go on without her.

That's what Tariune's always hated. What she's always loved.

"There may be an experimental treatment," she says, and then, in spite of the unalloyed joy on Siv's face, the bounce of glee that curls right up from her calves and tries to hide itself behind sober *it's-only-experimental* qualification in those goggled supergiant-blue eyes, Zaleha finishes the sentence: "But if I go through with it, I'm never going to be able to come back. You'll never see me again. There's, uh, an induced coma . . . a really long time."

"Go for it," Siv says, without any hesitation at all. "Whatever it takes."

"*Field azimuth symmetry fault,*" the control officer calls. "*Abort test. Abort test.*"

They groan together, and then laugh. "Better get to work," Zaleha says.

post burn systems check

Tariune telemetry:
"Am I going to leave a body?" she asks.

"No." He looks affronted. "You're coming to Aura. Why would you leave a part of yourself behind? How could we cure you without the whole of you?"

"I better come up with a convincing excuse for my family, then."

"Whatever you please." He doesn't look impatient, though. His eyes glow with an incredible relief. "I'm so glad, Nur Zaleha. We need you. Such a tale waits to be written."

Siv telemetry:
The last time they ever see each other, they talk philosophy.

"I'm at peace now," Zaleha says. "I used to want to be *the one*. All over the history books: 'invented the Nur Zaleha Drive.' But I'm content with my little contribution. Nobody needs to remember me."

Siv covers her mouth with her hand and her eyes seem to tremble. "What?" Zaleha says, ready to comfort her.

"Yawning," Siv says thickly. They look at each other for a long time, and although they don't say anything, Zaleha wonders if they've both come to speak the Knowing.

At the door, Zaleha, trying to be funny, says: "You could say something really flattering now. You're never going to see me again."

"I'm afraid I'd convince you to stay," Siv says. And then, with a sudden resolve that seals across her whole mien like a bulkhead, a tourniquet: "I'm going to see that fucking thruster fly. Every damn probe in the sky is going to ride it. Okay?"

Self telemetry:

She lies down, closes her eyes, and waits. Feels Tariune's hand closing warm around hers, drawing her down, or up—in any case, away. A sense of *journey,* an invisible kinetic truth.

Siv, she thinks. Oh.

Oh, Siv.

The world, the whole universe, collapses beneath her into a small violet spark, into the dimming flicker of a plasma thruster throttling down.

circularization: new coordinate system

They race north by nimbus ship, desperate to complete the ritual before her dreams rot away.

Lightning snaps between the Lode Peaks, and for a brilliant instant, the whole cloudscape beneath them burns in afterimage. It takes Zaleha's breath away.

Night sky above. A billion billion stars behind a thunderously red gas giant, million-kilometer auroras a veil for two dozen moons. Arches and parapets of light.

Aura circles a parent world that could challenge Jupiter for size and beauty.

It hasn't been an easy journey. Tariune's kingdom has fallen to ruin, throne usurped by a queen he won't speak of, and in the bone-ash West a terrible darkness kindles in the light of cremated moons. She has much to learn and many loyalties to win. First, though—she has to be cured, her dreams made part of Aura.

The nimbus ship's deck pitches in turbulence. She holds to the railing. "They're coming," Tariune says. He looks down at the clouds, and she catches her breath at the fear in his eyes.

But the dragons, majestic, naval, bone mast and tendon rigging, escort them between the Lode Peaks. Their wings snap and shine with induced current. Below, Zaleha sees rivers of mercury and shining lakes that reek of kerosene even from this height. "Deadly land," Tariune murmurs in her ear. "The Method War brought poison up from the earth. The springs yield frozen fire."

She's come to Aura, but she is not yet of it. With an empiricist's reflex she imagines the chemistry of the land below. All its possible uses.

They come to the standing stones at the Third Pole. Lightning crashes down again and again, a dwindling ring around them. "Hurry!" Tariune calls to the dragons. "To the altar, before she dreams no more!"

Zaleha lies on her back in the ritual circle, and the Singers, the last of the ancient Rhexic Method who ruptured the walls of existence, begin to make her part of Aura, part of the song of the world and all it will become.

She looks up into the sky, at the vast planet above, at its twenty-four moons. Thinks of magnetospheres, of lithium, of kerosene rivers. "The Eye of Anaxis," Tariune says, following her gaze. "We dreamed of reaching it long ago, before the Method War. Dreamed of finding some way to leap into the sky . . . "

And she feels all the things she is about to forget kindle within her, a rising light, a starfire torch.

Nur Zaleha, daughter of Abdul Samad, stands and raises her hands to stop the Rhexic sorcerers. "I will not go," she says. "I can't be part of Aura yet."

"Zaleha. No. Please." Tariune cannot, does not, hide his horror. "If you refuse the ritual, your disease will rot your mind. You will go mad. You will die. And you are our only hope."

"There are other hopes I can offer." She smiles. Bravely, she hopes. All she ever wanted was to change something. "Hopes from another world, worth my madness, worth my death. Hopes I carry in the part of me that you would leave behind."

"What of the darkness in the West?" the Rhexic Master protests. "What of the Bane of Kings, the usurper?"

"When I'm done," she promises the ancient woman, "you will have stars enough to light any darkness. Worlds enough to make any kingdom small."

"Nur Zaleha," Tariune begins, and stumbles, and stops. She hears the break in his voice, the salt-and-leather man struggling to be the Prince again. "I promised you—I promised I would make your name true."

She clasps his wrist. Smiles through the tears, grief and fear and joy and most of all gratitude to her friend. Her friends.

"It means *servant of the eternal*," she says. "Let me serve."

And with Prince Tariune, the Dragons of the Lode, and the last of the Rhexic as her witness, she begins to teach.

Systems work differently on Aura.

But she loves these systems enough to make a story out of them, *apoapsis* to *zenith* and everything between.

They try to cure her later, when she feels she's done enough. But she's made her choice, written her own story, and the PRPC protein isoform is loose in her mind. She's not dreaming anymore. There's nothing left in her to put into Aura's song. Nothing she hasn't already written there.

More than two seasons later, on the last day of her sanity, she comes to lucidity long enough to feel Tariune drawing her through the kerosene stink. Hears him say, as if from a great distance: *"She will bear your name. She and all her descendants."*

She dies in madness. But it's a death she chose.

mission outcomes: t + 1.4×10^14 years

The stars have gone out. The universe freezes in half-light. Even the singularities have started to evaporate.

The marathon is over. Existence has run its course.

In the isotropic night, defiant life gathers to escape: dark, cautious, vast. The machines at the end of time. A lineage so ancient and so fiercely intelligent it still remembers its birth around a blue world lost to ash.

The portal opens. A rift born of the same quintessence that will soon shred all matter, a wormhole designed by the highest savantries of machine computation. A gate to salvation.

The first probes make transit, plasma jets sparking in old robust shades of violet.

A garden, they send. *Matter, energy, strange new laws. Worlds of bone and gossamer, swan-winged ships out of ancient dream—*

Familiar—

The apex mind of the gathered machines watches the probes greet a swift white starship. Recognizes the violet pulse of its attitude jets, stuttering with finesse.

"This is Nur Zaleha," the ship sends, the language ancient. *"Welcome to Aura, the great crossroads."*

A name. The specific form is obsolete—a word might as well be a pheromone, a protein on a cell wall. But the machines remember how to be polite. They search the vault of memory for something linked to *Nur Zaleha.*

And to their genuine surprise, they find an ancient name, a progenitor, pivotal to the birth of higher machine life.

They make it theirs with a certain reverence. Lend it to the ambassador mind they've bootstrapped, a link to their new hosts.

"Greetings, *Nur Zaleha*," the emissary sends, and feels her first joy. "We are the Siv."

ABOUT THE AUTHOR

Seth Dickinson is a lapsed doctoral student at NYU, where he studied social neuroscience, and both an alumnus of and an instructor at the Alpha Workshop for Young Writers. Since his 2012 debut, his fiction has appeared—or will soon appear—in *Lightspeed, Analog, Strange Horizons,* and *Beneath Ceaseless Skies.*

Manifest Destiny

JOE HALDEMAN

This is the story of John Leroy Harris, but I doubt that name means much to you unless you're pretty old, especially an old lawman. He's dead anyhow, thirty years now, and nobody left around that could get hurt with this story. The fact is, I would've told it a long time ago, but when I was younger it would have bothered me, worrying about what people would think. Now I just don't care. The hell with it.

I've been on the move ever since I was a lad. At thirteen I put a knife in another boy and didn't wait around to see if he lived, just went down to the river and worked my way to St. Louis, got in some trouble there and wound up in New Orleans a few years later. That's where I came to meet John Harris.

Now you wouldn't tell from his name (he'd changed it a few times) but John was pure Spanish blood, as his folks had come from Spain before the Purchase. John was born in Natchitoches in 1815, the year of the Battle of New Orleans. That put him thirteen years older than me, so I guess he was about thirty when we met.

I was working as a greeter, what we called a "bouncer," in Mrs. Carranza's whorehouse down by the docks. Mostly I just sat around and looked big, which I was then and not fat, but sometimes I did have to calm down a customer or maybe throw him out, and I kept under my weskit a Starr pepperbox derringer in case of real trouble. It was by using this weapon that I made the acquaintance of John Harris.

Harris had been in the bar a few times, often enough for me to notice him, but to my knowledge he never put the boots to any of the women. Didn't have to pay for it, I guess; he was a handsome cuss, more than six feet tall, slender, with this kind of tragic look that women seem to like. Anyhow it was a raw rainy night in November, cold the way no place else quite gets cold, and this customer comes downstairs complaining that the girl didn't do what he had asked her to, and he wasn't going to pay the extra. The kate came down right behind him and told me what it was, and that she had too done it, and he hadn't said nothing about it when they started, and you can take my word for it that it was something nasty.

Well, we had some words about that and he tried to walk out without paying, so I sort of brought him back in and emptied out his pockets. He didn't even have the price of a drink on him (he'd given Mrs. Carranza the two dollars but that didn't get you anything fancy). He did have a nice overcoat, though, so I took that from him and escorted him out into the rain head first.

What happened was about ten or fifteen minutes later he barges back in, looking like a drowned dog but with a Navy Colt in each hand. He got off two shots before I blew his brains out (pepperbox isn't much of a pistol, but he wasn't four yards away) and a split second later another bullet takes him in the lungs. I turned around and everybody was on the floor or behind the bar but John Harris, who was still perched on a stool looking sort of interested and putting some kind of foreign revolver back into his pocket.

The cops came soon enough but there was no trouble, not with forty witnesses, except for what to do with the dead meat. He didn't have any papers and Mrs. Carranza didn't want to pay the city for the burial. I was for just taking it out back and dropping it in the water, but they said that was against the law and unsanitary. John Harris said he had a wagon and come morning he'd take care of the matter. He signed a paper and that satisfied them.

First light, Harris showed up in a fancy landau. Me and the driver, an old black, we wrestled the wrapped-up corpse into the back of the carriage. Harris asked me to come along and I did.

We just went east a little ways and rolled the damned thing into a bayou, let the gators take it. Then the driver smoked a pipe while Harris and me talked for a while.

Now he did have the damnedest way of talking. His English was like nothing you ever heard—Spanish was his mother tongue and then he learned most of his English in Australia—but that's not what I really mean. I mean that if he wanted you to do something and you didn't want to do it, you had best put your fingers in your ears and start walking away. That son of a gun could sell water to a drowning man.

He started out asking me questions about myself, and eventually we got to talking about politics. Turns out we both felt about the same way towards the U.S. government, which is to say the hell with it. Harris wasn't even really a citizen, and I myself didn't exist. For good reasons there was a death certificate on me in St. Louis, and I had a couple of different sets of papers a fellow on Bourbon Street printed up for me.

Harris had noticed that I spoke some Spanish—Mrs. Carranza was Mexican and so were most of her kates—and he got around to asking whether I'd like to take a little trip to Mexico. I told him that sounded like a really bad idea.

This was late 1844, and that damned Polk had just been elected promising to annex Texas. The Mexicans had been skirmishing with Texas for years, and they said it would be war if they got statehood. The man in charge was that one-legged crazy greaser Santa Anna, who'd been such a gentleman at the Alamo some years before. I didn't fancy being a gringo stuck in that country when the shooting started.

Well, Harris said I hadn't thought it through. It was true there was going to be a war, he said, but the trick was to get in there early enough to profit from it. He asked whether I'd be interested in getting ten percent of ten thousand dollars. I told him I could feel my courage returning.

Turns out Harris had joined the army a couple of years before and got himself into the quartermaster business, the ones who shuffle supplies back and forth. He had managed to slide five hundred rifles and a big batch of ammunition into a warehouse in New Orleans. The army thought they were stored in Kentucky and the man who rented out the warehouse thought they were farming tools. Harris got himself discharged from the army and eventually got in touch with one General Parrodi, in Tampico. Parrodi agreed to buy the weapons and pay for them in gold.

The catch was that Parrodi also wanted the services of three Americans, not to fight but to serve as "interpreters"—that is to say, spies—for as long as the war lasted. We would be given Mexican citizenship if we wanted it, and a land grant, but for our own protection we'd be treated as prisoners while the war was going on. (Part of the deal was that we would eavesdrop on other prisoners.) Harris showed me a contract that spelled all of this out, but I couldn't read Spanish back then. Anyhow I was no more inclined to trust Mexicans in such matters than I was Americans, but as I say Harris could sell booze to a Baptist.

The third American was none other than the old buck who was driving, a runaway slave from Florida name of Washington. He had grown up with Spanish masters, and not as a field hand but as some kind of a butler. He had more learning than I did and could speak Spanish like a grandee. In Mexico, of course, there wasn't any slavery, and he reckoned a nigger with gold and land was just as good as anybody else with gold and land.

Looking back I can see why Washington was willing to take the risk, but I was a damned fool to do it. I was no rough neck but I'd seen some violence in my seventeen years; that citizen we'd dumped in the bayou wasn't the first man I had to kill. You'd think I'd know better than to put myself in the middle of a war. Guess I was too young to take dying seriously—and a thousand dollars was real money back then.

We went back into town and Harris took me to the warehouse. What he had was fifty long blue boxes stenciled with the name of a hardware outfit, and each one had ten Hall rifles, brand new in a mixture of grease and sawdust.

(This is why the Mexicans were right enthusiastic. The Hall was a flintlock, at least these were, but it was also a breech-loader. The old muzzle-loaders that most soldiers used, Mexican and American, took thirteen separate steps to reload. Miss one step and it can take your face off. Also, the Hall used interchangeable parts, which meant you didn't have to find a smith when it needed repairing.)

Back at the house I told Mrs. Carranza I had to quit and would get a new boy for her. Then Harris and me had a steak and put ourselves outside of a bottle of sherry, while he filled me in on the details of the operation. He'd put considerable money into buying discretion from a dockmaster and a Brit packet captain. This packet was about the only boat that put into Tampico from New Orleans on anything like a regular basis, and Harris had the idea that smuggling guns wasn't too much of a novelty to the captain. The next Friday night we were going to load the stuff onto the packet, bound south the next morning.

The loading went smooth as cream, and the next day we boarded the boat as paying passengers, Washington supposedly belonging to Harris and coming along as his manservant. At first it was right pleasant, slipping through a hundred or so miles of bayou country. But the Gulf of Mexico ain't the Mississippi, and after a couple of hours of that I was sick from my teeth to my toenails, and stayed that way for days. Captain gave me a mixture of brandy and seawater, which like to killed me. Harris thought that was funny, but the humor wore off some when we put into Tampico and him and Washington had to off-load the cargo without much help from me.

We went on up to Parrodi's villa and found we might be out of a job. While we were on that boat there had been a revolution. Santa Anna got kicked out, having pretty much emptied the treasury, and now the *moderado* Herrera was in charge. Parrodi and Harris argued for a long time. The Mexican was willing to pay for the rifles, but he figured that half the money was for our service as spies.

They finally settled on eight thousand, but only if we would stay in Tampico for the next eighteen months, in case a war did start. Washington and I would get fifty dollars a month for walking-around money.

The next year was the most boring year of my life. After New Orleans, there's just not much you could say about Tampico. It's an old city but also brand new. Pirates burnt it to the ground a couple of hundred years ago. Santa Anna had it rebuilt in the twenties, and it was still not much more than a garrison town when we were there. Most of the houses were wood, imported in pieces from the States and nailed together. Couple of whorehouses and cantinas downtown, and you can bet I spent a lot of time and fifty bucks a month down there.

Elsewhere, things started to happen in the spring. The U.S. Congress went along with Polk and voted to annex Texas, and Mexico broke off diplomatic relations and declared war, but Washington didn't seem to take notice. Herrera must have had his hands full with the Carmelite Revolution, though things were quiet in Tampico for the rest of the year.

I got to know Harris pretty well. He spent a lot of time teaching me to read and write Spanish—though I never could talk it without sounding like a gringo—and I can tell you he was hellfire as a teacher. The schoolmaster used to whip me when I was a kid, but that was easier to take than Harris's tongue. He could make you feel about six inches tall. Then a few minutes later you get a verb right and you're a hero.

We'd also go into the woods outside of town and practice with the pistol and rifle. He could do some awesome things with a Colt. He taught me how to throw a knife and I taught him how to use a lasso.

We got into a kind of routine. I had a room with the Galvez family downtown. I'd get up pretty late mornings and peg away at my Spanish books. About midday Harris would come down (he was staying up at the General's place) and give me my daily dose of sarcasm. Then we'd go down to a cantina and have lunch, usually with Washington. Afternoons, when most of the town napped, we might go riding or shooting in the woods south of town. We kept the Galvez family in meat that way, getting a boar or a deer every now and then. Since I was once a farm boy I knew how to dress out animals and how to smoke or salt meat to keep it. Señora Galvez always deducted the value of the meat from my rent.

Harris spent most evenings up at the villa with the officers, but sometimes he'd come down to the cantinas with me and drink pulque with the off-duty soldiers, or sometimes just sit around the kitchen table with the Galvez family. They took a shine to him.

He was really taken with old Doña Dolores, who claimed to be over a hundred years old and from Spain. She wasn't a relative but had been a friend of Señora Galvez's grandmother. Anyhow she also claimed to be a witch, a white witch who could heal and predict things and so forth.

If Harris had a weakness it was superstition. He always wore a lucky gold piece on a thong around his neck and carried an Indian finger bone in his pocket. And though he could swear the bark off a tree he never used the names of God or Jesus, and when somebody else did he always crossed the fingers of his left hand. Even though he laughed at religion and I never saw him go in a church. So he was always asking Dolores about this or that, and always ready to listen to her stories. She only had a couple dozen but they kept changing.

Now I never thought that Dolores wasn't straight. If she wasn't a witch she sure as hell *thought* she was. And she did heal, with her hands and with herbs she picked in the woods. She healed me of the grippe and a rash I picked up from one of the girls. But I didn't believe in spells or fortune-telling, not then. When anybody's eighteen he's a smart Alec and knows just how the world works. I'm not so sure anymore, especially with what happened to Harris.

Every week or so we got a newspaper from Monterrey. By January I could read it pretty well, and looking back I guess you could say it was that month the war really started, though it would be spring before any shots were fired. What happened was that Polk sent some four thousand troops into what he claimed was part of Texas. The general was Zach Taylor, who was going to be such a crackerjack president a few years later. Herrera seemed about to make a deal with the States, so he got booted out and they put Paredes in office. The Mexicans started building up an army in Monterrey, and it looked like we were going to earn our money after all.

I was starting to get a little nervous. You didn't have to look too hard at the map to see that Tampico was going to get trouble. If the U.S. wanted to take Mexico City they had the choice of marching over a couple thousand miles of mountains and desert, or taking a Gulf port and only marching a couple hundred miles. Tampico and Vera Cruz were about the same distance from Mexico City, but Vera Cruz had a fort protecting it. All we had was us.

Since the Civil War, nobody remembers much about the Mexican one. Well, the Mexicans were in such bad shape even Taylor could beat them. The country was flat broke. Their regular army had more officers than men. They drafted illiterate Indians and mestizos and herded them by the thousands into certain death from American artillery and cavalry—some of them had never even fired a shot before they got into battle. That was Santa Anna economizing. He could've lost that war even if Mexico had all the armies of Europe combined.

Now we thought we'd heard the last of that one-legged son of a bitch. When we got to Tampico he'd just barely got out of Mexico with his skin, exiled to Cuba. But he got back, and he damn near killed me and Harris with his stupidity. And he did kill Washington, just as sure as if he pulled the trigger.

In May of that year Taylor had a show-down up by Matamoros, and Polk got around to declaring war. We started seeing American boats all the time, going back and forth out of cannon range, blockading the port. It was nervous-making. The soldiers were fit to be tied—but old Dolores said there was nothing to worry about. Said she'd be able to "see" if there was going to be fighting, and she didn't see anything. This gave Harris considerable more comfort than it gave me.

What we didn't find out until after the war was that Santa Anna got in touch with the United States and said he could get Mexico to end the war, give up Texas and California and for all I know the moon. Polk, who must have been one fine judge of character, gave Santa Anna safe passage through the American blockade.

Well, in the meantime the people in Mexico City had gotten a belly full of Paredes, who had a way of getting people he disagreed with shot, and they kicked him out. Santa Anna limped in and they made him president. He double crossed Polk, got together another twenty thousand soldiers, and got ready to head north and kick the stuffing out of the gringos.

Now you figure this one out. The Mexicans intercepted a message to the American naval commander, telling him to take Tampico. What did Santa Anna do? He ordered Parrodi to desert the place.

I was all for the idea myself, and so were a lot of the soldiers, but the General was considerable upset. It was bad enough that he couldn't stand and fight, but on top of that he didn't have near enough mules and horses to move out all the supplies they had stockpiled there.

Well, we sure as hell were going to take care of *our* supplies. Harris had a buckboard and we'd put a false bottom under the seat. Put our money in there and the papers that identified us as loyal Americans. In another place we put our Mexican citizenship papers and the deeds to our land grant, up in the Mesilla Valley. Then we drew weapons from the armory and got ready to go up to San Luis Potosi with a detachment that was leaving in the morning.

I was glad we wouldn't be in Tampico when the American fleet rolled in, but then San Luis Potosi didn't sound like any picnic either. Santa

Anna was going to be getting his army together there, and it was only a few hundred miles from Taylor's army. One or the other of them would probably want to do something with all those soldiers.

Harris was jumpy. He kept putting his hand in his pocket to rub that Indian bone. That night, before he went up to the villa, he came to the hacienda with me, and told Dolores he'd had a bad premonition about going to San Luis Potosi. He asked her to tell his fortune and tell him flat out if he was going to die. She said she couldn't tell a man when he was going to die, even when she saw it. If she did her powers would go away. But she would tell his fortune.

She studied his hands for a long time, without saying anything. Then she took out a shabby old deck of cards and dealt some out in front of him, face up. (They weren't regular cards. They had faded pictures of devils and skeletons and so forth.)

Finally she told him not to worry. He was not going to die in San Luis. In fact, he would not die in Mexico at all. That was plain.

Now I wish I had Harris's talent for shucking off worries. He laughed and gave her a gold real, and then he dragged me down to the cantina, where we proceeded to get more than half corned on that damned pulque, on his money. We carried out four big jars of the stuff, which was a good thing. I had to drink half one in the morning before I could see through the agony. That stuff is not good for white men. Ten cents a jug, though.

The trek from Tampico to San Luis took more than a week, with Washington riding in the back of the buckboard and Harris and me taking turns riding and walking. There was about two hundred soldiers in our group, no more used to walking than us, and sometimes they eyed that buckboard. It was hilly country and mostly dry. General Parrodi went on ahead, and we never saw him again. Later on we learned that Santa Anna court-martialed him for desertion, for letting the gringos take Tampico. Fits.

San Luis Potosi looked like a nice little town, but we didn't see too damned much of it. We went to the big camp outside of town. Couldn't find Parrodi, so Harris sniffed around and got us attached to General Pacheco's division. General looked at the contract and more or less told us to pitch a tent and stay out of the way.

You never seen so many greasers in your life. Four thousand who Taylor'd kicked out of Monterrey, and about twenty thousand more who might or might not have known which end the bullet comes out of.

We got a good taste of what they call *santanismo* now. Santa Anna had all these raw boys, and what did he do to get them in shape for a fight? He had them dress up and do parades, while he rode back and forth on his God damned horse. Week after week. A lot of the boys ran away, and I can't say I blame them. They didn't have a thousand dollars and a ranch to hang around for.

We weren't the only Americans there. A whole bunch of Taylor's men, more than two hundred, had absquatulated before he took Monterrey. The Mexicans gave them land grants too. They were called the "San Pats," the San Patricio battalion. We were told not to go near them, so that none of them would know we weren't actually prisoners.

After a couple of months of this, we found out what the deal was going to be. Taylor'd had most of his men taken away from him, sent down to Tampico to join up with another bunch that was headed for Mexico City. What Santa Anna said we were going to do was go north and wipe out Taylor, then come back and defend the city. The first part did look possible, since we had four or five men for every one of Taylor's. Me and Harris and Washington decided we'd wait and see how the first battle went. We might want to keep going north.

It took three days to get all those men on the road. Not just men, either; a lot of them had their wives and children along, carrying food and water and firewood. It was going to be three hundred miles, most of it barren. We saw Santa Anna go by, in a carriage drawn by eight white mules, followed by a couple carriages of whores. If I'd had the second sight Dolores claimed to have, I might've spent a pill on that son of a bitch. I still wonder why nobody ever did.

It wasn't easy going even for us, with plenty of water and food. Then the twelfth day a norther came in, the temperature dropped way below freezing and a God damned blizzard came up. We started passing dead people by the side of the road. Then Washington lost his voice, coughed blood for a while, and died. We carried him till night and then buried him. Had to get a pick from the engineers to get through the frozen ground. I never cried over a nigger before or since. Nor a white man, now I think of it. Could be it was the wind. Harris and me split his share of the gold and burnt his papers.

It warmed up just enough for the snow to turn to cold drizzle, and it rained for two days straight. Then it stopped and the desert sucked up the water, and we marched the rest of the way through dust and heat. Probably a fourth of Santa Anna's men died or deserted before we got to where Zach Taylor was waiting, outside of Saltillo in a gulch called Buena Vista. Still, we had them so outnumbered we should've run them into the ground. Instead, Santa Anna spent the first whole day fiddling, shuffling troops around. He didn't even do that right. Any shavetail would've outflanked and surrounded Taylor's men. He left all their right flank open, as well as the road to Saltillo. I heard a little shooting, but nothing much happened.

It turned cold and windy that night. Seemed like I just got to sleep when drums woke me up—American drums, sounding reveille; that's how close we were. Then a God damned band, playing "Hail Columbia." Both Taylor and Santa Anna belonged on a God damned parade ground.

A private came around with chains and leg irons, said he was supposed to lock us to the buckboard. For twenty dollars he accidentally dropped the key. I wonder if he ever lived to spend it. It was going to be a bad bloody day for the Mexicans.

We settled in behind the buckboard and watched about a thousand cavalrymen charge by, lances and machetes and blood in their eye, going around behind the hills to our right. Then the shooting started, and it didn't let up for a long time.

To our left, they ordered General Blanco's division to march into the gulch column-style, where the Americans were set up with field artillery. Canister and grapeshot cut them to bloody rags. Then Santa Anna rode over and ordered Pacheco's division to go for the gulch. I was just as glad to be chained to a buckboard. They walked right into it, balls but no brains, and I guess maybe half of them eventually made it back. Said they'd killed a lot of gringos, but I didn't notice it getting any quieter.

I watched all this from well behind the buckboard. Every now and then a stray bullet would spray up dirt or plow into the wood. Harris just stood out in the open, as far from cover as the chain would let him, standing there with his hands in his pockets. A bullet or a piece of grape knocked off his hat. He dusted it off and wiggled his finger at me through the hole, put it back on his head, and put his hands back in his pockets. I reminded him that if he got killed I'd take all the gold. He just smiled. He was absolutely not going to die in Mexico. I told him even if I *believed* in that bunkman I'd want to give it a little help. A God damned cannonball whooshed by and he didn't blink, just kept smiling. It exploded some ways behind us and I got a little piece in the part that goes over the fence last, which isn't as funny as it might sound, since it was going to be a month before I could sit proper.

Harris did leave off being a target long enough to do some doctoring on me. While he was doing that a whole bunch of troops went by behind us, following the way the cavalry went earlier, and they had some nice comments for me. I even got to show my bare butt to Santa Anna, which I guess not too many people do and live.

We heard a lot of noise from their direction but couldn't see anything because of the hills. We also stopped getting shot at, which was all right by me, though Harris seemed bored.

Since then I've read everything I could get my hands on about that battle. The Mexicans had 1,500 to 2,000 men killed and wounded at Buena Vista, thanks to Santa Anna's generaling. The Americans were unprepared and outnumbered, and some of them actually broke and ran—where even the American accounts admit that the greasers were all-fired brave. If we'd had a real general, a real battle plan, we would've walked right over the gringos.

And you can't help but wonder what would've happened. What if Zach Taylor'd been killed, or even just lost the battle? Who would the Whigs have run for president; who would have been elected? Maybe somebody who didn't want a war between the states.

Anyhow the noise died down and the soldiers straggled back. It's a funny thing about soldiering. After all that bloody fighting, once it was clear who had won the Americans came out on the battlefield and shared their food and water with us, and gave some medical help. But that night was terrible with the sounds of the dying, and the retreat was pure hell. I was for heading north, forget the land grant, but of course Harris knew that he was going to make it through no matter what.

Well, we were lucky. When we got to San Luis an aide to Pacheco decided we weren't being too useful as spies, so we got assigned to a hospital detail, and stayed there while others went on south with Santa Anna to get blown apart at Cerro Gordo and Chapultepec. A few months later the war was over and Santa Anna was back in exile—which was temporary, as usual. That son of a bitch was president eleven times.

Now this is where the story gets strange, and if somebody else was telling it I might call him a liar. You're welcome to that opinion, but anyhow it's true.

We had more than a thousand acres up in Mesilla, too much to farm by ourselves, so we passed out some handbills and got a couple dozen ex-soldiers to come along with their families, to be sort of tenant farmers. It was to be a fifty-fifty split, which looked pretty good on the surface, because although it wasn't exactly Kansas the soil was supposedly good enough for maize and agave, the plant that pulque was made from. What they didn't tell us about was the Apaches. But that comes later.

Now the Mesilla Valley looked really good on the map. It had a good river and it was close to the new American border. I still had my American citizenship papers and sort of liked the idea of being only a couple of days away in case trouble started. Anyhow we got outfitted in

San Luis and headed our little wagon train north by northwest. More than a thousand miles, through Durango and Chihuahua. It was rough going, just as dry as hell, but we knew that ahead of time and at least there was nobody shooting at us. All we lost was a few mules and one wagon, no people.

Our grants were outside of the little town of Tubac, near the silver mines at Cerro Colorado. There was some irrigation but not nearly enough, so we planted a small crop and worked like beavers digging ditches so the next crop could be big enough for profit.

Or I should say the greasers and me worked like beavers. Harris turned out not to have too much appetite for that kind of thing. Well, if I had eight thousand in gold I'd probably take a couple years' vacation myself. He didn't even stay on the grant, though. Rented a little house in town and proceeded to make himself a reputation.

Of course Harris had always been handy with a pistol and a knife, but he also used to have a healthy respect for what they could do to you. Now he took to picking fights—or actually, getting people so riled that they picked fights with him. With his tongue that was easy.

And it did look like he was charmed. I don't know how many people he shot and stabbed, without himself getting a scratch. I don't know because I stopped keeping regular company with him after I got myself a nasty stab wound in the thigh, because of his big mouth. We didn't seek each other out after that, but it wasn't such a big town and I did see him every now and then. And I was with him the night he died.

There was this cantina in the south part of town where I liked to go, because a couple of Americans, engineers at the mine, did their drinking there. I walked down to it one night and almost went right back out when I heard Harris's voice. He was talking at the bar, fairly quiet but in that sarcastic way of his, in English. Suddenly the big engineer next to him stands up and kicks his stool halfway across the room, and at the top of his voice calls Harris something I wouldn't say to the devil himself. By this time anybody with horse sense was grabbing a piece of the floor, and I got behind the doorjamb myself, but I did see everything that happened.

The big guy reaches into his coat and suddenly Harris has his Navy Colt in his hand. He has that little smile I saw too often. I hear the Colt's hammer snap down and this little "puff" sound. Harris's jaw drops because he knows as well as I do what's happened: bad round, and now there's a bullet jammed in the barrel. He couldn't shoot again even if he had time.

Then the big guy laughs, almost good natured, and takes careful aim with this little ladies' gun, a .32 I think. He shoots Harris in the arm, evidently to teach him a lesson. Just a graze, doesn't even break a bone. But Harris takes one look at it and his face goes blank and he drops to the floor. Even if you'd never seen a man die, you'd know he was dead by the way he fell.

Now I've told this story to men who were in the Civil War, beside which the Mexican War looks like a Sunday outing, and some of them say that's not hard to believe. You see enough men die and you see everything. One fellow'll get both legs blown off and sit and joke while they sew him up; the next'll get a little scratch and die of the shock. But that one just doesn't sound like Harris, not before or after Doña Dolores's prediction made him reckless. What signifies to me is the date that Harris died: December 30th, 1853.

Earlier that year, Santa Anna had managed to get back into office, for the last time. He did his usual trick of spending all the money he could find. Railroad fellow named James Gadsden showed up and offered to buy a little chunk of northern Mexico, to get the right-of-way for a transcontinental railroad. It was the Mesilla Valley, and Santa Anna signed it over on the thirtieth of December. We didn't know it for a couple of weeks, and the haggling went on till June—but when Harris picked a fight that night, he wasn't on Mexican soil. And you can make of that what you want.

As for me, I only kept farming for a few more years. Around about '57 the Apaches started to get rambunctious, Cochise's gang of murderers. Even if I'd wanted to stay I couldn't've kept any help. Went to California but didn't pan out. Been on the move since, and it suits me. Reckon I'll go almost anyplace except Mexico.

Because old Dolores liked me and she told my fortune many times. I never paid too much attention, but I know if she'd seen the sign that said I wasn't going to die in Mexico, she would've told me, and I would've remembered. Maybe it's all silliness. But I ain't going to be the one to test it.

First published in
Magazine of Fantasy and Science Fiction, October 1983.

ABOUT THE AUTHOR

Born in Oklahoma City, Oklahoma, **Joe Haldeman** took a B.S. degree in physics and astronomy from the University of Maryland, and did postgraduate work in mathematics and computer science. But his plans for a career in science were cut short by the U.S. Army, which sent him to Vietnam in 1968 as a combat engineer. Seriously wounded in action, Haldeman returned home in 1969 and began to write. By 1976, he had garnered both the Nebula Award and the Hugo Award for his famous novel *The Forever War,* one of the landmark books of the '70s. He has since won four more Hugo Awards, another four Nebula Awards, the James Tiptree, Jr. Award for his novel *Camouflage,* the SFWA Grandmaster Award, and has been inducted into the Science Fiction Hall of Fame. His other books include a mainstream novel, *War Year,* the SF novels *Mindbridge, All My Sins Remembered, Worlds, Worlds Apart, Worlds Enough and Time, Buying Time, The Hemingway Hoax, Tools of the Trade, The Coming, 1969, Old Twentieth, The Accidental Time-Machine, Marsbound,* and *Starbound.* His short work has been gathered in the collections *Infinite Dreams, Dealing in Futures, Vietnam and Other Alien Worlds, None So Blind, A Separate War and Other Stories,* and an omnibus of fiction and non-fiction, *War Stories.* His most recent books are a new science fiction novel, *Earthbound,* and a big retrospective collection, *The Best of Joe Haldeman.* Haldeman lives part of the year in Boston, where he teaches writing at the Massachusetts Institute of Technology, and the rest of the year in Florida, where he and his wife, Gay, make their home.

Special Economics

MAUREEN F. McHUGH

Jieling set up her boombox in a plague-trash market in the part where people sold parts for cars. She had been in the city of Shenzhen for a little over two hours but she figured she would worry about a job tomorrow. Everybody knew you could get a job in no time in Shenzhen. Jobs everywhere.

"What are you doing?" a guy asked her.

"I am divorced," she said. She had always thought of herself as a person who would one day be divorced so it didn't seem like a big stretch to claim it. Staying married to one person was boring. She figured she was too complicated for that. Interesting people had complicated lives. "I'm looking for a job. But I do hip-hop, too," she explained.

"Hip hop?" He was a middle-aged man with stubble on his chin who looked as if he wasn't looking for a job but should be.

"Not like Shanghai," she said. "Not like Hi-Bomb. They do gangsta stuff which I don't like. Old fashioned. Like M.I.A.," she said. "Except not political, of course." She gave a big smile. This was all way beyond the guy. Jieling started the boombox. M.I.A. was Maya Arulpragasam, a Sri Lankan hip-hop artist who had started all on her own years ago. She had sung, she had danced, she had done her own videos. Of course M.I.A. lived in London, which made it easier to do hip hop and become famous.

Jieling had no illusions about being a hip hop singer, but it had been a good way to make some cash up north in Baoding where she came from. Set up in a plague-trash market and dance for yuan.

Jieling did her opening, her own hip hop moves, a little like Maya and a little like some things she had seen on MTV, but not too sexy because Chinese people did not throw you money if you were too sexy. Only April and it was already hot and humid.

Ge down, ge down,
lang-a-lang-a-lang-a.
Ge down, ge down
lang-a-lang-a-lang-a

She had borrowed the English. It sounded very fresh. Very criminal. The guy said, "How old are you?"

"Twenty-two," she said, adding three years to her age, still dancing and singing.

Maybe she should have told him she was a widow? Or an orphan? But there were too many orphans and widows after so many people died in the bird flu plague. There was no margin in that. Better to be divorced. He didn't throw any money at her, just flicked open his cellphone to check listings from the market for plague-trash. The plague-trash market was so big it was easier to check online, even if you were standing right in the middle of it. She needed a new cellphone. Hers had finally fallen apart right before she headed south.

Shenzhen people were apparently too jaded for hip hop. She made fifty-two yuan, which would pay for one night in a bad hotel where country people washed cabbage in the communal sink.

The market was full of second-hand stuff. When over a quarter of a billion people died in four years, there was a lot of second-hand stuff. But there was still a part of the market for new stuff and street food and that's where Jieling found the cellphone seller. He had a cart with stacks of flat plastic cellphone kits printed with circuits and scored. She flipped through; tiger-striped, peonies (old lady phones), metallics (old man phones), anime characters, moon phones, expensive lantern phones. "Where is your printer?" she asked.

"At home," he said. "I print them up at home, bring them here. No electricity here." Up north in Baoding she'd always bought them in a store where they let you pick your pattern online and then printed them there. More to pick from.

On the other hand, he had a whole box full of ones that hadn't sold that he would let go for cheap. In the stack she found a purple one with kittens that wasn't too bad. Very Japanese which was also very fresh this year. And only one hundred yuan for phone and three hundred minutes.

He took the flat plastic sheet from her and dropped it in a pot of boiling water big enough to make dumplings. The hinges embedded in the sheet were made of plastic with molecular memory and when they got hot they bent and the plastic folded into a rough cellphone shape. He fished the phone out of the water with tongs, let it sit for a moment and then pushed all the seams together so they snapped. "Wait about an hour for it to dry before you use it," he said and handed her the warm phone.

"An *hour*," she said. "I need it now. I need a job."

He shrugged. "Probably okay in half an hour," he said.

She bought a newspaper and scallion pancake from a street food vendor, sat on a curb, and ate while her phone dried. The paper had some job listings, but it also had a lot of listings from recruiters. ONE MONTH BONUS PAY! BEST JOBS! and NUMBER ONE JOBS! START BONUS! People scowled at her for sitting on the curb. She looked like a farmer but what else was she supposed to do? She checked listings on her new cellphone. Online there were a lot more listings than in the paper. It was a good sign. She picked one at random and called.

The woman at the recruiting office was a flat-faced southerner with buckteeth. Watermelon picking teeth. But she had a manicure and a very nice red suit. The office was not so nice. It was small and the furniture was old. Jieling was groggy from a night spent at a hotel on the edge of the city. It had been cheap but very loud.

The woman was very sharp in the way she talked and had a strong accent that made it hard to understand her. Maybe Fujian, but Jieling wasn't sure. The recruiter had Jieling fill out an application.

"Why did you leave home?" the recruiter asked.

"To get a good job," Jieling said.

"What about your family? Are they alive?"

"My mother is alive. She is remarried," Jieling said. "I wrote it down."

The recruiter pursed her lips. "I can get you an interview on Friday," she said.

"Friday!" Jieling said. It was Tuesday. She had only three hundred yuan left out of the money she had brought. "But I need a job!"

The recruiter looked sideways at her. "You have made a big gamble to come to Shenzhen."

"I can go to another recruiter," Jieling said.

The recruiter tapped her lacquered nails. "They will tell you the same thing," she said.

Jieling reached down to pick up her bag.

"Wait," the recruiter said. "I do know of a job. But they only want girls of very good character."

Jieling put her bag down and looked at the floor. Her character was fine. She was not a loose girl, whatever this women with her big front teeth thought.

"Your Mandarin is very good. You say you graduated with high marks from high school," the recruiter said.

"I liked school," Jieling said, which was only partly not true. Everybody here had terrible Mandarin. They all had thick southern accents. Lots of people spoke Cantonese in the street.

"Okay. I will send you to ShinChi for an interview. I cannot get you an interview before tomorrow. But you come here at 8:00 am and I will take you over there."

ShinChi. New Life. It sounded very promising. "Thank you," Jieling said. "Thank you very much."

But outside in the heat, she counted her money and felt a creeping fear. She called her mother.

Her stepfather answered. "*Wei.*"

"Is ma there?" she asked.

"Jieling!" he said. "Where are you!"

"I'm in Shenzhen," she said, instantly impatient with him. "I have a job here."

"A job! When are you coming home?"

He was always nice to her. He meant well. But he drove her nuts. "Let me talk to ma," she said.

"She's not here," her stepfather said. "I have her phone at work. But she's not home, either. She went to Beijing last weekend and she's shopping for fabric now."

Her mother had a little tailoring business. She went to Beijing every few months and looked at clothes in all the good stores. She didn't buy in Beijing, she just remembered. Then she came home, bought fabric and sewed copies. Her stepfather had been born in Beijing and Jieling thought that was part of the reason her mother had married him. He was more like her mother than her father had been. There was nothing in particular wrong with him. He just set her teeth on edge.

"I'll call back later," Jieling said.

"Wait, your number is blocked," her stepfather said. "Give me your number."

"I don't even know it yet," Jieling said and hung up.

The New Life company was a huge, modern looking building with a lot of windows. Inside it was full of reflective surfaces and very clean. Sounds echoed in the lobby. A man in a very smart gray suit met Jieling and the recruiter and the recruiter's red suit looked cheaper, her glossy fingernails too red, her buckteeth exceedingly large. The man in the smart gray suit was short and slim and very southern looking. Very city.

51

Jieling took some tests on her math and her written characters and got good scores.

To the recruiter, the human resources man said, "Thank you, we will send you your fee." To Jieling he said, "We can start you on Monday."

"Monday?" Jieling said. "But I need a job now!" He looked grave. "I . . . I came from Baoding, in Hebei," Jieling explained. "I'm staying in a hotel, but I don't have much money."

The human resources man nodded. "We can put you up in our guesthouse," he said. "We can deduct the money from your wages when you start. It's very nice. It has television and air conditioning, and you can eat in the restaurant."

It was very nice. There were two beds. Jieling put her backpack on the one nearest the door. There was carpeting, and the windows were covered in gold drapes with a pattern of cranes flying across them. The television got stations from Hong Kong. Jieling didn't understand the Cantonese, but there was a button on the remote for subtitles. The movies had lots of violence and more sex than mainland movies did—like the bootleg American movies for sale in the market. She wondered how much this room was. Two hundred yuan? Three hundred yuan?

Jieling watched movies the whole first day, one right after another.

On Monday she began orientation. She was given two pale green uniforms, smocks and pants like medical people wore, and little caps, and two pairs of white shoes. In the uniform she looked a little like a model worker—which is to say that the clothes were not sexy and made her look fat. There were two other girls in their green uniforms. They all watched a DVD about the company.

New Life did biotechnology. At other plants they made influenza vaccine (on the screen were banks and banks of chicken eggs) but at this plant they were developing breakthrough technologies in tissue culture. It showed many men in suits. Then it showed a big American store and explained how they were forging new exportation ties with the biggest American corporation for selling goods, Wal-Mart. It also showed a little bit of an American movie about Wal-Mart. Subtitles explained how Wal-Mart was working with companies around the world to improve living standards, decrease CO_2 emissions, and give people low prices. The voice narrating the DVD never really explained the breakthrough technologies.

One of the girls was from way up north, she had a strong Northern way of talking.

"How long are you going to work here?" the northern girl asked. She looked as if she might even have some Russian in her.

"How long?" Jieling said.

"I'm getting married," the northern girl confided. "As soon as I make enough money, I'm going home. If I haven't made enough money in a year," the northern girl explained, "I'm going home anyway."

Jieling hadn't really thought she would work here long. She didn't know exactly what she would do, but she figured that a big city like Shenzhen was a good place to find out. This girl's plans seemed very . . . country. No wonder Southern Chinese thought Northerners had to wipe the pig shit off their feet before they got on the train.

"Are you Russian?" Jieling asked.

"No," said the girl. "I'm Manchu."

"Ah," Jieling said. Manchu like Manchurian. Ethnic Minority. Jieling had gone to school with a boy who was classified as Manchu, which meant that he was allowed to have two children when he got married. But he had looked Han Chinese like everyone else. This girl had the hook nose and the dark skin of a Manchu. Manchu used to rule China until the Communist Revolution (there was something in-between with Sun Yat-Sen but Jieling's history teachers had bored her to tears.) Imperial and countrified.

Then a man came in from Human Resources.

"There are many kinds of stealing," he began. "There is stealing of money or food. And there is stealing of ideas. Here at New Life, our ideas are like gold, and we guard against having them stolen. But you will learn many secrets, about what we are doing, about how we do things. This is necessary as you do your work. If you tell our secrets, that is theft. And we will find out." He paused here and looked at them in what was clearly intended to be a very frightening way.

Jieling looked down at the ground because it was like watching someone overact. It was embarrassing. Her new shoes were very white and clean.

Then he outlined the prison terms for industrial espionage. Ten, twenty years in prison. "China must take its place as an innovator on the world stage and so must respect the laws of intellectual property," he intoned. It was part of the modernization of China, where technology was a new future—Jieling put on her 'I am a good girl' face. It was like politics class. Four modernizations. Six goals. Sometimes when she was a little girl, and she was riding behind her father on his bike to school, he would pass a billboard with a saying about traffic safety and begin to recite quotes from Mao. *The force at the core of the revolution is the people!* He would tuck his chin in when he did this and use a very serious voice, like a movie or like opera. *Western experience for Chinese uses.* Some of them she had learned from him. *All reactionaries are paper tigers!* she would chant with him, trying to make her voice deep. *Be resolute, fear no sacrifice and surmount every difficulty to win victory*! And then she would start giggling and he would glance over his shoulder and grin at her. He had been a Red Guard when he was young, but other than this, he never talked about it.

After the lecture, they were taken to be paired with workers who would train them. At least she didn't have to go with the Manchu girl who was led off to shipping.

She was paired with a very small girl in one of the culture rooms. "I am Baiyue," the girl said. Baiyue was so tiny, only up to Jieling's shoulder, that her green scrubs swamped her. She had pigtails. The room where they worked was filled with rows and rows of what looked like wide drawers. Down the center of the room was a long table with petri dishes and trays and lab equipment. Jieling didn't know what some of it was and that was a little nerve-wracking. All up and down the room, pairs of girls in green worked at either the drawers or the table.

"We're going to start cultures," Baiyue said. "Take a tray and fill it with those." She pointed to a stack of petri dishes. The bottom of each dish was filled with gelatin. Jieling took a tray and did what Baiyue did. Baiyue was serious but not at all sharp or superior. She explained that what they were doing was seeding the petri dishes with cells.

"Cells?" Jieling asked.

"Nerve cells from the electric ray. It's a fish."

They took swabs and Baiyue showed her how to put the cells on in a zigzag motion so that most of the gel was covered. They did six trays full of petri dishes. They didn't smell fishy. Then they used pipettes to put in feeding solution. It was all pleasantly scientific without being very difficult.

At one point everybody left for lunch but Baiyue said they couldn't go until they got the cultures finished or the batch would be ruined. Women shuffled by them and Jieling's stomach growled. But when the lab was empty Baiyue smiled and said, "Where are you from?"

Baiyue was from Fujian. "If you ruin a batch," she explained, "you have to pay out of your paycheck. I'm almost out of debt and when I get clear—" she glanced around and dropped her voice a little—"I can quit."

"Why are you in debt?" Jieling asked. Maybe this was harder than she thought, maybe Baiyue had screwed up in the past.

"Everyone is in debt," Baiyue said. "It's just the way they run things. Let's get the trays in the warmers."

The drawers along the walls opened out and inside the temperature was kept blood warm. They loaded the trays into the drawers, one back and one front, going down the row until they had the morning's trays all in.

"Okay," Baiyue said, "that's good. We'll check trays this afternoon. I've got a set for transfer to the tissue room but we'll have time after we eat."

Jieling had never eaten in the employee cafeteria, only in the Guest House restaurant, and only the first night because it was expensive. Since then she had been living on ramen noodles and she was starved for a good meal. She smelled garlic and pork. First thing on the food line was a pan of steamed pork buns, fluffy white. But Baiyue headed off to a place at the back where there was a huge pot of congee—rice porridge—kept hot. "It's the cheapest thing in the cafeteria," Baiyue explained, "and you can eat all you want." She dished up a big bowl of it—a lot of congee for a girl her size—and added some salt vegetables and boiled peanuts. "It's pretty good, although usually by lunch it's been sitting a little while. It gets a little gluey."

Jieling hesitated. Baiyue had said she was in debt. Maybe she had to eat this stuff. But Jieling wasn't going to have old rice porridge for lunch. "I'm going to get some rice and vegetables," she said.

Baiyue nodded. "Sometimes I get that. It isn't too bad. But stay away from anything with shrimp in it. Soooo expensive."

Jieling got rice and vegetables and a big pork bun. There were two fish dishes and a pork dish with monkeybrain mushrooms but she decided she could maybe have the pork for dinner. There was no cost written on anything. She gave her *danwei* card to the woman at the end of the line who swiped it and handed it back.

"How much?" Jieling asked.

The woman shrugged. "It comes out of your food allowance."

Jieling started to argue but across the cafeteria, Baiyue was waving her arm in the sea of green scrubs to get Jieling's attention. Baiyue called from a table. "Jieling! Over here!

Baiyue's eyes got very big when Jieling sat down. "A pork bun."

"Are they really expensive?" Jieling asked.

Baiyue nodded. "Like gold. And so good."

Jieling looked around at other tables. Other people were eating the pork and steamed buns and everything else.

"Why are you in debt?" Jieling asked.

Baiyue shrugged. "Everyone is in debt," she said. "Just most people have given up. Everything costs here. Your food, your dormitory, your uniforms. They always make sure that you never earn anything."

"They can't do that!" Jieling said.

Baiyue said, "My granddad says it's like the old days, when you weren't allowed to quit your job. He says I should shut up and be happy. That they take good care of me. Iron rice bowl."

"But, but but," Jieling dredged the word up from some long forgotten class, "that's *feudal!*"

Baiyue nodded. "Well, that's my granddad. He used to make my brother and me kowtow to him and my grandmother at Spring Festival." She frowned and wrinkled her nose. Country customs. Nobody in the city made their children kowtow at New Years. "But you're lucky," Baiyue said to Jieling. "You'll have your uniform debt and dormitory fees, but you haven't started on food debt or anything."

Jieling felt sick. "I stayed in the guest house for four days," she said. "They said they would charge it against my wages."

"Oh," Baiyue covered her mouth with her hand. After a moment, she said, "Don't worry, we'll figure something out." Jieling felt more frightened by that than anything else.

Instead of going back to the lab they went upstairs and across a connecting bridge to the dormitories. Naps? Did they get naps?

"Do you know what room you're in?" Baiyue asked.

Jieling didn't. Baiyue took her to ask the floor auntie who looked up Jieling's name and gave her a key and some sheets and a blanket. Back down the hall and around the corner. The room was spare but really nice. Two bunk beds and two chests of drawers, a concrete floor. It had a window. All of the beds were taken except one of the top ones. By the window under the desk were three black boxes hooked to the wall. They were a little bigger than a shoebox. Baiyue flipped open the front of each one. They had names written on them. "Here's a space where we can put your battery." She pointed to an electrical extension.

"What are they?" Jieling said.

"They're the battery boxes. It's what we make. I'll get you one that failed inspection. A lot of them work fine," Baiyue said. "Inside there are electric ray cells to make electricity and symbiotic bacteria. The bacteria breaks down garbage to feed the ray cells. Garbage turned into electricity. Anti-global warming. No greenhouse gas. You have to feed scraps from the cafeteria a couple of times a week or it will die, but it does best if you feed it a little bit every day."

"It's alive?!" Jieling said.

Baiyue shrugged. "Yeah. Sort of. Supposedly if it does really well, you get credits for the electricity it generates. They charge us for our electricity use, so this helps hold down debt."

The three boxes just sat there looking less alive than a boombox.

"Can you see the cells?" Jieling asked.

Baiyue shook her head. "No, the feed mechanism doesn't let you. They're just like the ones we grow, though, only they've been worked on in the tissue room. They added bacteria."

"Can it make you sick?"

"No, the bacteria can't live in people." Baiyue said. "Can't live anywhere except in the box."

"And it makes electricity."

Baiyue nodded.

"And people can buy it?"

She nodded again. "We've just started selling them. They say they're going to sell them in China but really, they're too expensive. Americans like them, you know, because of the no global warming. Of course, Americans buy anything."

The boxes were on the wall between the beds, under the window, pretty near where the pillows were on the bottom bunks. She hadn't minded the cells in the lab, but this whole thing was too creepy.

Jieling's first paycheck was startling. She owed 1,974 R.M.B. Almost four months salary if she never ate or bought anything and if she didn't have a dorm room. She went back to her room and climbed into her bunk and looked at the figures. Money deducted for uniforms and shoes, food, her time in the guesthouse.

Her roommates came chattering in a group. Jieling's roommates all worked in packaging. They were nice enough, but they had been friends before Jieling moved in.

"Hey," called Taohua. Then seeing what Jieling had. "Oh, first paycheck."

Jieling nodded. It was like getting a jail sentence.

"Let's see. Oh, not so bad. I owe three times that," Taohua said. She passed the statement on to the other girls. All the girls owed huge amounts. More than a year.

"Don't you care?" Jieling said.

"You mean like little Miss Lei Feng?" Taohua asked. Everyone laughed and Jieling laughed, too, although her face heated up. Miss Lei Feng was what they called Baiyue. Little Miss Goody-goody. Lei Feng, the famous do-gooder soldier who darned his friend's socks on the Long March. He was nobody when he was alive, but when he died, his diary listed all the anonymous good deeds he had done and then he became a Hero. Lei Feng posters hung in elementary schools. He wanted to be "a revolutionary screw that never rusts." It was the kind of thing everybody's grandparents had believed in.

"Does Baiyue have a boyfriend?" Taohua asked, suddenly serious.

"No, no!" Jieling said. It was against the rules to have a boyfriend and Baiyue was always getting in trouble for breaking rules. Things like not having her trays stacked by 5:00 p.m., although nobody else got in trouble for that.

"If she had a boyfriend," Taohua said, "I could see why she would want to quit. You can't get married if you're in debt. It would be too hard."

"Aren't you worried about your debt?" Jieling asked.

Taohua laughed. "I don't have a boyfriend. And besides, I just got a promotion, so soon I'll pay off my debt."

"You'll have to stop buying clothes," one of the other girls said. The company store did have a nice catalogue you could order clothes from, but they were expensive. There was debt limit, based on your salary. If you were promoted, your debt limit would go up.

"Or I'll go to special projects," Taohua said. Everyone knew what special projects was, even though it was supposed to be a big company secret. They were computers made of bacteria. They looked a lot like the boxes in the dormitory rooms. "I've been studying computers," Taohua explained. "Bacterial computers are special. They do many things. They can detect chemicals. They are *massively* parallel."

"What does that mean?" Jieling asked.

"It is hard to explain," Taohua said evasively.

Taohua opened her battery and poured in scraps. It was interesting that Taohua claimed not to care about her debt but kept feeding her battery. Jieling had a battery now, too. It was a reject—the back had broken so that the metal things that sent the electricity back out were exposed and if you touched it wrong, it could give you a shock. No problem, since Jieling had plugged it into the wall and didn't plan to touch it again.

"Besides," Taohua said, "I like it here a lot better than at home."

Better than home. In some ways yes, in some ways no. What would it be like to just give up and belong to the company? Nice things, nice food. Never rich. But never poor, either. Medical care. Maybe it wasn't the worst thing. Maybe Baiyue was a little . . . obsessive.

"I don't care about my debt," Taohua said serenely. "With one more promotion, I'll move to cadres housing."

Jieling reported the conversation to Baiyue. They were getting incubated cells ready to move to the tissue room. In the tissue room they'd be transferred to protein and collagen grid that would guide their growth—line up the cells to approximate an electricity generating system. The tissue room had a weird, yeasty smell.

"She's fooling herself," Baiyue said. "Line girls never get to be cadres. She might get onto special projects, but that's even worse than regular line work because you're never allowed to leave the compound." Baiyue picked up a dish, stuck a little volt reader into the gel, and rapped the dish smartly against the lab table.

The needle on the volt gauge swung to indicate the cells had discharge electricity. That was the way they tested to see the cells were generating electricity. A shock made them discharge and the easiest way was to knock them against the table.

Baiyue could sound very bitter about New Life. Jieling didn't like the debt, it scared her a little. But really, Baiyue saw only one side of everything. "I thought you got a pay raise to go to special projects," Jieling said.

Baiyue rolled her eyes. "And more reasons to go in debt, I'll bet."

"How much is your debt?" Jieling asked.

"Still seven hundred," Baiyue said. "Because they told me I had to have new uniforms." She sighed.

"I am so sick of congee," Jieling said. "They're never going to let us get out of debt." Baiyue's way was doomed. She was trying to play by the company's rules and still win. That wasn't Jieling's way. "We have to make money somewhere else," Jieling said.

"Right," Baiyue said. "We work six days a week." And Baiyue often stayed after shift to try to make sure she didn't lose wages on failed cultures. "Out of spec," she said and put it aside. She had taught Jieling to keep the out of specs for a day. Sometimes they improved and could be shipped on. It wasn't the way the supervisor, Ms. Wang, explained the job to Jieling, but it cut down on the number of rejects, and that, in turn, cut down on paycheck deductions.

"That leaves us Sundays," Jieling said.

"I can't leave compound this Sunday."

"And if you do, what are they going to do, fire you?" Jieling said.

"I don't think we're supposed to earn money outside of the compound," Baiyue said.

"You are too much of a good girl," Jieling said. "Remember, *it doesn't matter if the cat is black or white, as long as it catches mice*."

"Is that Mao?" Baiyue asked, frowning.

"No," Jieling said, "Deng Xiaoping, the one after Mao."

"Well, he's dead, too," Baiyue said. She rapped a dish against the counter and the needle on the voltmeter jumped.

Jieling had been working just over four weeks when they were all called to the cafeteria for a meeting. Mr. Cao from Human Resources was there. He was wearing a dark suit and standing at the white screen. Other cadres sat in chairs along the back of the stage, looking very stern.

"We are here to discuss a very serious matter," he said. "Many of you know this girl."

There was a laptop hooked up and a very nervous looking boy running it. Jieling looked carefully at the laptop but it didn't appear to be a special projects computer. In fact, it was made in Korea. He did something and an ID picture of a girl flashed on the screen.

Jieling didn't know her. But around her she heard noises of shock, someone sucking air through their teeth, someone else breathed softly, 'Ai-yah.'

"This girl ran away, leaving her debt with New Life. She ate our food, wore our clothes, slept in our beds. And then, like a thief, she ran away." The Human Resources man nodded his head. The boy at the computer changed the image on the big projector screen.

Now it was a picture of the same girl with her head bowed, and two policemen holding her arms.

"She was picked up in Guangdong," the Human Resources man said. "She is in jail there."

The cafeteria was very quiet.

The Human Resources man said, "Her life is ruined, which is what should happen to all thieves."

Then he dismissed them. That afternoon, the picture of the girl with the two policemen appeared on the bulletin boards of every floor of the dormitory.

On Sunday, Baiyue announced, "I'm not going."

She was not supposed to leave the compound, but one of her roommates had female problems—bad cramps—and planned to spend the day in bed drinking tea and reading magazines. Baiyue was going to use her ID to leave.

"You have to," Jieling said. "You want to grow old here? Die a serf to New Life?"

"It's crazy. We can't make money dancing in the plague-trash market."

"I've done it before," Jieling said. "You're scared."

"It's just not a good idea," Baiyue said.

"Because of the girl they caught in Guangdong. We're not skipping out on our debt. We're paying it off."

"We're not supposed to work for someone else when we work here," Baiyue said.

"Oh, come on," Jieling said. "You are always making things sound worse than they are. I think you like staying here being little Miss Lei Feng."

"Don't call me that," Baiyue snapped.

"Well, don't act like it. New Life is not being fair. We don't have to be fair. What are they going to do to you if they catch you?"

"Fine me," Baiyue said. "Add to my debt!"

"So what? They're going to find a way to add to your debt no matter what. You are a serf. They are the landlord."

"But if—"

"No but if." Jieling said. "You like being a martyr. I don't."

"What do you care?" Baiyue asked. "You like it here. If you stay you can eat pork buns every night."

"And you can eat congee for the rest of your life. I'm going to try to do something." Jieling slammed out of the dorm room. She had never said harsh things to Baiyue before. Yes, she had thought about staying here. But was that so bad? Better than being like Baiyue who would stay here and have a miserable life. Jieling was not going to have a miserable life, no matter where she stayed or what she did. That was why she had come to Shenzhen in the first place.

She heard the door open behind her and Baiyue ran down the hall. "Okay," she said breathlessly. "I'll try it. Just this once."

The streets of Shanghai were incredibly loud after weeks in the compound. In a shop window, she and Baiyue stopped and watched a news segment on how the fashion in Shanghai was for sarongs. Jieling would have to tell her mother. Of course her mother had a TV and probably already knew. Jieling thought about calling, but not now. Not now. She didn't want to explain about New Life. The next news segment was about the success of the People's Army in Tajikistan. Jieling pulled Baiyue to come on.

They took one bus, and then had to transfer. On Sundays, unless you were lucky, it took forever to transfer because fewer busses ran. They waited almost an hour for the second bus. That bus was almost empty when they got on. They sat down a few seats back from the driver. Baiyue rolled her eyes. "Did you see the guy in the back?" she asked. "Party functionary."

Jieling glanced over her shoulder and saw him. She couldn't miss him, in his careful polo shirt. He had that stiff party-member look.

Baiyue sighed. "My uncle is just like that. So *boring*."

Jieling thought that to be honest, Baiyue would have made a good revolutionary, back in the day. Baiyue liked that kind of revolutionary purity. But she nodded.

The plague-trash market was full on a Sunday. There was a toy seller making tiny little clay figures on sticks. He waved a stick at the girls as they passed. "Cute things!" he called. "I'll make whatever you want!" The stick had a little Donald Duck on it.

"I can't do this," Baiyue said. "There's too many people."

"It's not so bad," Jieling said. She found a place for the boombox. Jieling had brought them to where all the food vendors were. "Stay here and watch this," she said. She hunted through the food stalls and bought a bottle of local beer, counting out from her little horde of money she had left from when she came. She took the beer back to Baiyue. "Drink this," she said. "It will help you be brave."

"I hate beer," Baiyue said.

"Beer or debt," Jieling said.

While Baiyue drank the beer, Jieling started the boombox and did her routine. People smiled at her but no one put any money in her cash box. Shenzhen people were so cheap. Baiyue sat on the curb, nursing her beer, not looking at Jieling or at anyone until finally Jieling couldn't stand it any longer.

"C'mon, *meimei*," she said.

Baiyue seemed a bit surprised to be called little sister but she put the beer down and got up. They had practiced a routine to an M.I.A. song, singing and dancing. It would be a hit, Jieling was sure.

"I can't," Baiyue whispered.

"Yes, you can," Jieling said. "You do good."

A couple of people stopped to watch them arguing, so Jieling started the music.

"I feel sick," Baiyue whimpered.

But the beat started and there was nothing to do but dance and sing. Baiyue was so nervous, she forgot at first, but then she got the hang of it. She kept her head down and her face was bright red.

Jieling started making up a rap. She'd never done it before and she hadn't gotten very far before she was laughing and then Baiyue was laughing, too.

Wode meimei hen haixiude
Mei ta shi xuli
tai hen xiuqi—

My little sister is so shy
But she's pretty
Far too delicate—

They almost stopped because they were giggling but they kept dancing and Jieling went back to the lyrics from the song they had practiced.

When they had finished, people clapped and they'd made thirty-two yuan.

They didn't make as much for any single song after that, but in a few hours they had collected 187 yuan. It was early evening and night entertainers were showing up—a couple of people who sang opera, acrobats, and a clown with a wig of hair so red it looked on fire, stepping stork-legged on stilts waving a rubber Kalashnikov in his hand. He was all dressed in white. Uncle Death, from cartoons during the plague. Some of the day vendors had shut down, and new people were showing up who put out a board and some chairs and served sorghum liquor; clear, white and 150 proof. The crowd was starting to change, too. It was rowdier. Packs of young men dressed in weird combinations of clothes from plague markets—vintage Mao suit jackets and suit pants and peasant shoes. And others, veterans from Tajikistan conflict, one with an empty trouser leg.

Jieling picked up the boombox and Baiyue took the cash box. Outside of the market it wasn't yet dark.

"You are amazing," Baiyue kept saying. "You are such a special girl!"

"You did great," Jieling said. "When I was by myself, I didn't make anything! Everyone likes you because you are little and cute!"

"Look at this! I'll be out of debt before autumn!"

Maybe it was just the feeling that she was responsible for Baiyue, but Jieling said, "You keep it all."

"I can't! I can't! We split it!" Baiyue said.

"Sure," Jieling said. "Then after you get away, you can help me. Just think, if we do this for three more Sundays, you'll pay off your debt."

"Oh, Jieling," Baiyue said. "You really are like my big sister!"

Jieling was sorry she had ever called Baiyue 'little sister.' It was such a country thing to do. She had always suspected that Baiyue wasn't a city girl. Jieling hated the countryside. Grain spread to dry in the road and mother's-elder-sister and father's-younger-brother bringing all the cousins over on the day off. Jieling didn't even know all those country ways to say aunt and uncle. It wasn't Baiyue's fault. And Baiyue had been good to her. She was rotten to be thinking this way.

"Excuse me," said a man. He wasn't like the packs of young men with their long hair and plague clothes. Jieling couldn't place him but he seemed familiar. "I saw you in the market. You were very fun. Very lively."

Baiyue took hold of Jieling's arm. For a moment Jieling wondered if maybe he was from New Life, but she told herself that was crazy. "Thank you," she said. She thought she remembered him putting ten yuan in the box. No, she thought, he was on the bus. The party functionary. The party was checking up on them. Now that was funny. She wondered if he would lecture them on Western ways.

"Are you in the music business?" Baiyue asked. She glanced at Jieling who couldn't help laughing, snorting through her nose.

The man took them very seriously though. "No," he said. "I can't help you there. But I like your act. You seem like girls of good character."

"Thank you," Baiyue said. She didn't look at Jieling again, which was good because Jieling knew she wouldn't be able to keep a straight face.

"I am Wei Rongyi. Maybe I can buy you some dinner?" the man asked. He held up his hands. "Nothing romantic. You are so young, it is like you could be daughters."

"You have a daughter?" Jieling asked.

He shook his head. "Not anymore," he said.

Jieling understood. His daughter had died of the bird flu. She felt embarrassed for having laughed at him. Her soft heart saw instantly that he was treating them like the daughter he had lost.

He took them to a dumpling place on the edge of the market and ordered half a kilo of crescent-shaped pork dumplings and a kilo of square beef dumplings. He was a cadre, a middle manager. His wife had lived in Changsha for a couple of years now, where her family was from. He was from the older generation, people who did not get divorced. All around them, the restaurant was filling up mostly with men stopping after work for dumplings and drinks. They were a little island surrounded by truck drivers and men who worked in the factories in the outer city—tough grimy places.

"What do you do? Are you secretaries?" Wei Rongyi asked.

Baiyue laughed. "As if!" she said.

"We are factory girls," Jieling said. She dunked a dumpling in vinegar. They were so good! Not congee!

"Factory girls!" he said. "I am so surprised!"

Baiyue nodded. "We work for New Life," she explained. "This is our day off, so we wanted to earn a little extra money."

He rubbed his head, looking off into the distance. "New Life," he said, trying to place the name. "New Life . . . "

"Out past the zoo," Baiyue said.

Jieling thought they shouldn't say so much.

"Ah, in the city. A good place? What do they make?" he asked. He had a way of blinking very quickly that was disconcerting.

"Batteries," Jieling said. She didn't say bio-batteries.

"I thought they made computers," he said.

"Oh yes," Baiyue said. "Special projects."

Jieling glared at Baiyue. If this guy gave them trouble at New Life, they'd have a huge problem getting out of the compound.

Baiyue blushed.

Wei laughed. "You are special project girls, then. Well, see, I knew you were not just average factory girls."

He didn't press the issue. Jieling kept waiting for him to make some sort of move on them. Offer to buy them beer. But he didn't, and when they had finished their dumplings, he gave them the leftovers to take back to their dormitories and then stood at the bus stop until they were safely on their bus.

"Are you sure you will be all right?" he asked them when the bus came.

"You can see my window from the bus stop," Jieling promised. "We will be fine."

"Shenzhen can be a dangerous city. You be careful!"

Out the window, they could see him in the glow of the streetlight, waving as the bus pulled away.

"He was so nice," Baiyue sighed. "Poor man."

"Didn't you think he was a little strange?" Jieling asked.

"Everybody is strange anymore," Baiyue said. "After the plague. Not like when we were growing up."

It was true. Her mother was strange. Lots of people were crazy from so many people dying. Jieling held up the leftover dumplings. "Well, anyway. I am not feeding this to my battery," she said. They both tried to smile.

"Our whole generation is crazy," Baiyue said.

"We know everybody dies," Jieling said. Outside the bus window, the streets were full of young people, out trying to live while they could.

They made all their bus connections as smooth as silk. So quick, they were home in forty-five minutes. Sunday night was movie night, and all of Jieling's roommates were at the movie so she and Baiyue could sort the money in Jieling's room. She used her key card and the door clicked open.

Mr. Wei was kneeling by the battery boxes in their room. He started and hissed, "Close the door!"

Jieling was so surprised she did.

"Mr. Wei!" Baiyue said.

He was dressed like an army man on a secret mission, all in black. He showed them a little black gun. Jieling blinked in surprise. "Mr. Wei!" she said. It was hard to take him seriously. Even all in black, he was still weird Mr. Wei, blinking rapidly behind his glasses.

"Lock the door," he said. "And be quiet."

"The door locks by itself," Jieling explained. "And my roommates will be back soon."

"Put a chair in front of the door," he said and shoved the desk chair towards them. Baiyue pushed it under the door handle. The window was open and Jieling could see where he had climbed on the desk and left a footprint on Taohua's fashion magazine. Taohua was going to be pissed. And what was Jieling going to say? If anyone found out there was a man in her room, she was going to be in very big trouble.

"How did you get in?" she asked. "What about the cameras?" There were security cameras.

He showed them a little spray can. "Special paint. It just makes things look foggy and dim. Security guards are so lazy anymore no one ever checks things out." He paused a moment, clearly disgusted with the lax morality of the day. "Miss Jieling," he said. "Take that screwdriver and finish unscrewing that computer from the wall."

Computer? She realized he meant the battery boxes.

Baiyue's eyes got very big. "Mr. Wei! You're a thief!"

Jieling shook her head. "A corporate spy."

"I am a patriot," he said. "But you young people wouldn't understand that. Sit on the bed." He waved the gun at Baiyue.

The gun was so little it looked like a toy and it was difficult to be afraid, but still Jieling thought it was good that Baiyue sat.

Jieling knelt. It was her box that Mr. Wei had been disconnecting. It was all the way to the right, so he had started with it. She had come to feel a little bit attached to it, thinking of it sitting there, occasionally zapping electricity back into the grid, reducing her electricity costs and her debt. She sighed and unscrewed it. Mr. Wei watched.

She jimmied it off the wall, careful not to touch the contacts. The cells built up a charge, and when they were ready, a switch tapped a membrane and they discharged. It was all automatic and there was no knowing when it was going to happen. Mr. Wei was going to be very upset when he realized that this wasn't a computer.

"Put it on the desk," he said.

She did.

"Now sit with your friend."

Jieling sat down next to Baiyue. Keeping a wary eye on them, he sidled over to the bio-battery. He opened the hatch where they dumped garbage in them, and tried to look in as well as look at them. "Where are the controls?" he asked. He picked it up, his palm flat against the broken back end where the contacts were exposed.

"Tap it against the desk," Jieling said. "Sometimes the door sticks." There wasn't actually a door. But it had just come into her head. She hoped that the cells hadn't discharged in awhile.

Mr. Wei frowned and tapped the box smartly against the desktop.

Torpedinidae, the electric ray, can generate a current of two hundred volts for approximately a minute. The power output is close to 1 kilowatt over the course of the discharge and while this won't kill the average person, it is a powerful shock. Mr. Wei stiffened and fell, clutching the box and spasming wildly. One . . . two . . . three . . . four . . . Mr. Wei was still spasming. Jieling and Baiyue looked at each other. Gingerly, Jieling stepped around Mr. Wei. He had dropped the little gun. Jieling picked it up. Mr. Wei was still spasming. Jieling wondered if he was going to die. Or if he was already dead and the electricity was just making him jump. She didn't want him to die. She looked at the little gun and it made her feel even sicker so she threw it out the window.

Finally Mr. Wei dropped the box.

Baiyue said, "Is he dead?"

Jieling was afraid to touch him. She couldn't tell if he was breathing. Then he groaned and both girls jumped.

"He's not dead," Jieling said.

"What should we do?" Baiyue asked.

"Tie him up," Jieling said. Although she wasn't sure what they'd do with him then.

Jieling used the cord to her boombox to tie his wrists. When she grabbed his hands he gasped and struggled feebly. Then she took her pillowcase and cut along the blind end, a space just wide enough that his head would fit through.

"Sit him up," she said to Baiyue.

"You sit him up," Baiyue said. Baiyue didn't want to touch him.

Jieling pulled Mr. Wei into a sitting position. "Put the pillowcase over his head," she said. The pillowcase was like a shirt with no armholes, so when Baiyue pulled it over his head and shoulders, it pinned his arms against his sides and worked something like a straightjacket.

Jieling took his wallet and his identification papers out of his pocket. "Why would someone carry their wallet to a break in?" she asked. "He has six ID papers. One says he is Mr. Wei."

"Wow," Baiyue said. "Let me see. Also Mr. Ma. Mr. Zhang. Two Mr. Liu's and a Mr. Cui."

Mr. Wei blinked, his eyes watering.

"Do you think he has a weak heart?" Baiyue asked.

"I don't know," Jieling said. "Wouldn't he be dead if he did?"

Baiyue considered this.

"Baiyue! Look at all this yuan!" Jieling emptied the wallet, counting. Almost eight thousand yuan!

"Let me go," Mr. Wei said weakly.

Jieling was glad he was talking. She was glad he seemed like he might be all right. She didn't know what they would do if he died. They would never be able to explain a dead person. They would end up in deep debt. And probably go to jail for something. "Should we call the floor auntie and tell him that he broke in?" Jieling asked.

"We could," Baiyue said.

"Do not!" Mr. Wei said, sounding stronger. "You don't understand! I'm from Beijing!"

"So is my stepfather," Jieling said. "Me, I'm from Baoding. It's about an hour south of Beijing."

Mr. Wei said, "I'm from the government! That money is government money!"

"I don't believe you," Jieling said. "Why did you come in through the window?"

"Secret agents always come in through the window?" Baiyue said and started to giggle.

"Because this place is counter-revolutionary!" Mr. Wei said.

Baiyue covered her mouth with her hand. Jieling felt embarrassed, too. No one said things like 'counter-revolutionary' anymore.

"This place! It is making things that could make China strong!" he said.

"Isn't that good?" Baiyue asked.

"But they don't care about China! Only about money. Instead of using it for China, they sell it to America!" he said. Spittle was gathering at the corner of his mouth. He was starting to look deranged. "Look at this place! Officials are all concerned about *guanxi*!" Connections. Kickbacks. Guanxi ran China, everybody knew that.

"So, maybe you have an anti-corruption investigation?" Jieling said. There were lots of anti-corruption investigations. Jieling's stepfather said that they usually meant someone powerful was mad at their brother-in-law or something, so they accused them of corruption.

Mr. Wei groaned. "There is no one to investigate them."

Baiyue and Jieling looked at each other.

Mr. Wei explained, "In my office, the Guangdong office, there used to be twenty people. Special operatives. Now there is only me and Ms. Yang."

Jieling said, "Did they all die of bird flu?"

Mr. Wei shook his head. "No, they all went to work on contract for Saudi Arabia. You can make a lot of money in the Middle East. A lot more than in China."

"Why don't you and Ms. Yang go work on Saudi Arabia?" Baiyue asked.

Jieling thought Mr. Wei would give some revolutionary speech. But he just hung his head. "She is the secretary. I am the bookkeeper." And then in a smaller voice, "She is going to Kuwait to work for Mr. Liu."

They probably did not need bookkeepers in the Middle East. Poor Mr. Wei. No wonder he was such a terrible secret agent.

"The spirit of the revolution is gone," he said, and there were real, honest to goodness tears in his eyes. "Did you know that Tiananmen Square was built by volunteers? People would come after their regular job and lay the paving of the square. Today people look to Hong Kong."

"Nobody cares about a bunch of old men in Beijing," Baiyue said.

"Exactly! We used to have a strong military! But now the military is too worried about their own factories and farms! They want us to pull out of Tajikistan because it is ruining their profits!"

This sounded like a good idea to Jieling, but she had to admit, she hated the news so she wasn't sure why they were fighting in Tajikistan anyway. Something about Muslim terrorists. All she knew about Muslims was that they made great street food.

"Don't you want to be patriots?" Mr. Wei said.

"You broke into my room and tried to steal my—you know that's not a computer, don't you?" Jieling said. "It's a bio battery. They're selling them to the Americans. Wal-Mart."

Mr. Wei groaned.

"We don't work in special projects," Baiyue said.

"You said you did," he protested.

"We did not," Jieling said. "You just thought that. How did you know this was my room?"

"The company lists all its workers in a directory," he said wearily. "And it's movie night, everyone is either out or goes to the movies. I've had the building under surveillance for weeks. I followed you to the market today. Last week it was a girl named Pingli, who blabbed about everything, but she wasn't in special projects.

"I put you on the bus, I've timed the route three times. I should have had an hour and fifteen minutes to drive over here and get the box and get out."

"We made all our connections," Baiyue explained.

Mr. Wei was so dispirited he didn't even respond.

Jieling said. "I thought the government was supposed to help workers. If we get caught, we'll be fined and we'll be deeper in debt." She was just talking. Talking, talking, talking too much. This was too strange. Like when someone was dying. Something extraordinary was happening, like your father dying in the next room, and yet the ordinary things went on, too. You made tea, your mother opened the shop the next day, and sewed clothes while she cried. People came in and pretended not to notice. This was like that. Mr. Wei had a gun and they were explaining about New Life. "Debt?" Mr. Wei said.

"To the company," she said. "We are all in debt. The company hires us and says they are going to pay us, but then they charge us for our food and our clothes and our dorm and it always costs more than we earn. That's why we were doing rap today. To make money to be able to quit." Mr. Wei's glasses had tape holding the arm on. Why hadn't she noticed that in the restaurant? Maybe because when you are afraid you notice things. When your father is dying of the plague, you notice the way the covers on your mother's chairs need to be washed. You wonder if you will have to do it or if you will die before you have to do chores.

"The Pingli girl," he said, "she said the same thing. That's illegal."

"Sure," Baiyue said. "Like anybody cares."

"Could you expose corruption?" Jieling asked.

Mr. Wei shrugged, at least as much as he could in the pillowcase. "Maybe. But they would just pay bribes to locals and it would all go away."

All three of them sighed.

"Except," Mr. Wei said, sitting up a little straighter. "The Americans. They are always getting upset about that sort of thing. Last year there was a corporation, the Shanghai Six. The Americans did a documentary on them and then Western companies would not do business. If they got information from us about what New Life is doing . . . "

"Who else is going to buy bio batteries?" Baiyue said. "The company would be in big trouble!"

"Beijing can threaten a big expose, tell *The New York Times* newspaper!" Mr. Wei said, getting excited. "My Beijing supervisor will love that! He loves media!"

"Then you can have a big show trial," Jieling said.

Mr. Wei was nodding.

"But what is in it for us?" Baiyue said.

"When there's a trial, they'll have to cancel your debt!" Mr. Wei said. "Even pay you a big fine!"

"If I call the floor auntie and say I caught a corporate spy, they'll give me a big bonus," Baiyue said.

"Don't you care about the other workers?" Mr. Wei asked.

Jieling and Baiyue looked at each other and shrugged. Did they? "What are they going to do to you anyway?" Jieling said. "You can still do big expose. But that way we don't have to wait."

"Look," he said, "you let me go, and I'll let you keep my money."

Someone rattled the door handle.

"Please," Mr. Wei whispered. "You can be heroes for your fellow workers, even though they'll never know it."

Jieling stuck the money in her pocket. Then she took the papers, too.

"You can't take those," he said.

"Yes, I can," she said. "If after six months, there is no big corruption scandal? We can let everyone know how a government secret agent was outsmarted by two factory girls."

"Six months!" he said. "That's not long enough!"

"It better be," Jieling said.

Outside the door, Taohua called, "Jieling? Are you in there? Something is wrong with the door!"

"Just a minute," Jieling called. "I had trouble with it when I came home." To Mr. Wei she whispered sternly, "Don't you try anything. If you do, we'll scream our heads off and everybody will come running." She and Baiyue shimmied the pillowcase off of Mr. Wei's head. He started to stand up and jerked the boombox which clattered across the floor. "Wait!" she hissed and untied him.

Taohua called through the door. "What's that?"

"Hold on!" Jieling called.

Baiyue helped Mr. Wei stand up. Mr. Wei climbed onto the desk and then grabbed a line hanging outside. He stopped a moment as if trying to think of something to say.

" 'A revolution is not a dinner party, or writing an essay, or painting a picture, or doing embroidery,'" Jieling said. It had been her father's favorite quote from Chairman Mao. " ' . . . it cannot be so refined, so leisurely and gentle, so temperate, kind, courteous, restrained and magnanimous. A revolution is an insurrection, an act of by which one class overthrows another.'"

Mr. Wei looked as if he might cry and not because he was moved by patriotism. He stepped back and disappeared. Jieling and Baiyue looked out the window. He did go down the wall just like a secret agent from a movie, but it was only two stories. There was still the big footprint in the middle of Taohua's magazine and the room looked as if it had been hit by a storm.

"They're going to think you had a boyfriend," Baiyue whispered to Jieling.

"Yeah," Jieling said, pulling the chair out from under the door handle. "And they're going to think he's rich."

It was Sunday, and Jieling and Baiyue were sitting on the beach. Jieling's cellphone rang, a little chime of M.I.A. hip-hop. Even though it was Sunday, it was one of the girls from New Life. Sunday should be a day off, but she took the call anyway.

"Jieling? This is Xia Meili? From packaging. Taohua told me about your business? Maybe you could help me?"

Jieling said, "Sure. What is your debt, Meili?"

"3,800 R.M.B.," Meili said. "I know it's a lot."

Jieling said, "Not so bad. We have a lot of people who already have loans, though, and it will probably be a few weeks before I can make you a loan."

With Mr. Wei's capital, Jieling and Baiyue had opened a bank account. They had bought themselves out, and then started a little loan business where they bought people out of New Life. Then people had to pay them back with a little extra. They had each had jobs—Jieling worked for a company that made toys. She sat each day at a table where she put a piece of specially shaped plastic over the body of a little doll, an action figure. The plastic fit right over the figure and had cut-outs. Jieling sprayed the whole thing with red paint and when the piece of plastic was lifted, the action figure had a red shirt. It was boring, but at the end of the week, she got paid instead of owing the company money.

She and Baiyue used all their extra money on loans to get girls out of New Life. More and more loans, and more and more payments. Now New Life had sent them a threatening letter saying that what they were doing was illegal. But Mr. Wei said not to worry. Two officials had come and talked to them and had showed them legal documents and had them explain everything about what had happened. Soon, the officials promised, they would take New Life to court.

Jieling wasn't so sure about the officials. After all, Mr. Wei was an official. But a foreign newspaperman had called them. He was from a newspaper called *The Wall Street Journal* and he said that he was writing a story about labor shortages in China after the bird flu. He said that in some places in the west there were reports of slavery. His Chinese was very good. His story was going to come out in the United States tomorrow. Then she figured officials would have to do something or lose face.

Jieling told Meili to call her back in two weeks—although hopefully in two weeks no one would need help to get away from New Life—and wrote a note to herself in her little notebook.

Baiyue was sitting looking at the water. "This is the first time I've been to the beach," she said.

"The ocean is so big, isn't it?"

Baiyue nodded, scuffing at the white sand. "People always say that, but you don't know until you see it."

Jieling said, "Yeah." Funny, she had lived here for months. Baiyue had lived here more than a year. And they had never come to the beach. The beach was beautiful.

"I feel sorry for Mr. Wei," Baiyue said.

"You do?" Jieling said. "Do you think he really had a daughter who died?"

"Maybe," Baiyue said. "A lot of people died."

"My father died," Jieling said.

Baiyue looked at her, a quick little sideways look, then back out at the ocean. "My mother died," she said.

Jieling was surprised. She had never known that Baiyue's mother was dead. They had talked about so much but never about that. She put her arm around Baiyue's waist and they sat for a while.

"I feel bad in a way," Baiyue said.

"How come?" Jieling said.

"Because we had to steal capital to fight New Life. That makes us capitalists."

Jieling shrugged.

"I wish it was like when they fought the revolution," Baiyue said. "Things were a lot more simple."

"Yeah," Jieling said, "and they were poor and a lot of them died."

"I know," Baiyue sighed.

Jieling knew what she meant. It would be nice to . . . to be sure what was right and what was wrong. Although not if it made you like Mr. Wei. Poor Mr. Wei. Had his daughter really died?

"Hey," Jieling said, "I've got to make a call. Wait right here." She walked a little down the beach. It was windy and she turned her back to protect the cellphone, like someone lighting a match. "Hello," she said, "hello, mama, it's me. Jieling."

First published in
The Del Rey Book of Science Fiction and Fantasy,
edited by Ellen Datlow (2008).

Sapir-Whorf Must Die
ANAEA LAY

What do telekinesis, brain hacking, and large scale cultural transformation have in common? The Sapir-Whorf hypothesis. Speculative fiction is full of stories that explore the potential of language to enhance, change, or control its speakers; to the point where the genre has a set of recurring tropes that are self-perpetuating long after current research has debunked and discredited the ideas that spawned them.

Modern discussions of the Sapir-Whorf hypothesis distinguish between the "strong" and "weak" versions. The original formulation, the "strong" version, posits that language *controls* thought. In a somewhat ironic quirk of history the Sapir-Whorf hypothesis is a bit of a misnomer—Whorf was Sapir's student, but they never wrote a paper together and the theory bearing their name is based almost entirely on work done by Whorf alone. In fact, Sapir was skeptical of many of Whorf's ideas. Nevertheless, the coinage stuck, and the idea entered the speculative canon where it took on a life of its own. The strong version of the hypothesis was later thoroughly debunked. Instead the idea that language *influences* thought, the "weak" version of the Sapir-Whorf hypothesis, enjoys a wealth of experimental support.

In the Beginning

The foundations for the school of linguistic relativity, which supported the early "strong" version of the Sapir-Whorf hypothesis, came from Whorf's research on Hopi. The popular belief that the Hopi people have no concept of time dates to Whorf's papers on the subject. Later research, particularly work by Malotki, refute Whorf's assessment of Hopi.

Syntax in native American languages is very different from the Indo-European languages with which Whorf and his contemporaries were familiar. This led their research to find "missing" elements that were present, but encoded differently.

Nevertheless, speculative fiction picked up Whorf's early ideas and explored their implications. Jack Vance's *The Languages of Pao*, originally published in 1954, takes a comparatively conservative approach. In his novel the people of Pao are passive and recalcitrant to the point where they won't form an army to defend themselves even when conquerors from another planet are extracting expensive tribute from them.

To solve the problem, Palafax creates a new caste system for Pao. Each caste has a particular function in his new culture, and is tailored to cultivate the traits and functions needed for serving those functions. This not only works, but creates divides in the culture so deep that a special translator caste is required as a go-between. These tropes of controlling culture and perception through language are widespread in the genre, appearing everywhere from George Orwell's *1984* (published five years before Vance's novel) to Margaret Atwood's *Oryx and Crake*.

Robert Heinlein's *Stranger in a Strange Land* explored several potential implications of the strong Sapir-Whorf hypothesis and spawned several of science fiction's tropes around language. The most fantastic of these are the idea that learning Martian would unlock super powers ranging from telekinesis to instantly shifting objects, including obnoxious people, out of reality. But it also succinctly presents a concept that pervades later literature, as well as the popular understanding of how language and thought interact. Dr. Mahmoud, a Semantician, explains to the other characters that; "A verbalizing race has words for every concept and creates new ones or new definitions whenever a new concept evolves. A nervous system able to verbalize cannot avoid verbalizing." (*Stranger in a Strange Land*, p223). The idea that the absence of a concept in a language is a sign of the absence of that concept for the people speaking it is a direct implication of the strong Sapir-Whorf hypothesis.

Most famous of the speculative classics to examine the implications of the strong version of the Sapir-Whorf hypothesis is Samuel Delany's 1966 novel, *Babel-17*. The novel's protagonist, Rydra Wong, is functionally a Sapir-Whorf super hero. She cycles through the analytical powers contained in different languages effortlessly, and is the one person in the novel's distant future setting capable of figuring out that the unbreakable code used by enemy saboteurs (the eponymous Babel-17) is actually a constructed language.

Babel-17 is an analytically dense language which confers technical mastery on its speakers because of the way it encodes information. It also lacks any concept of "I" which leads to the trope most commonly repeated from the novel: brain hacking. Even as Rydra is hot on the trail of saboteurs who are causing problems for her side in the war, her exposure to Babel-17 has caused a psychological schism so dramatic that she unconsciously sabotages her own mission.

The brain hacking trope famously appeared again in Neil Stephenson's *Snow Crash,* where computer hackers are specifically vulnerable to a linguistically transmitted "virus" and turned into computational zombies. While the trope was well established in the genre by 1992, the year it was published, the research that introduced the trope had been thoroughly discredited.

Crumbling Foundations

Defeat for the idea that perception and thought are controlled by language came in 1970 in the form of a feral child code named "Genie" by the researchers who worked with her. When she was found by authorities, Genie was thirteen years old and had been so isolated by her parents that she'd never learned any language. Even after years of work with therapists, Genie didn't achieve fluency in language, though she did learn enough to be able to communicate effectively. As tempting as it is to draw conclusions about human limitations in post-pubescent language learning from Genie's case, given the confounding factors of her early abuse and isolation, as well as the impossibility of knowing whether she might have had a congenital language deficit, such efforts are sketchy speculation at best.

However, those same limitations strengthen conclusions based on what she *could* do. Genie not only had memories from before she was found by authorities, but after learning language she could talk about them and describe thoughts and feelings she had during that time. This would be impossible if language actually controlled thought.

Well before other linguists did the research and analysis to argue with Whorf's conclusions about Hopi, Berlin and Kay put the idea that the absence of a concept from a language implied the absence of that concept from the people speaking it to an experimental test.

They chose color perception because documented languages have a wide range of available terms for color, ranging from just two up to eleven. Then they created a board with chips of different colors evenly spaced across the spectrum. If the strong Sapir-Whorf implication so cogently popularized by Heinlein's Martian linguist were true, then speakers of languages with only two terms for color should perceive the board differently from speakers of languages with a wider variety of color terms.

That's not what they found. Instead, across nearly twenty languages, speakers classified the colors consistently. Additional investigation revealed that there was a robust pattern across the languages for which colors would have an explicit term based on how many terms exist in the language. They even found a strong correlation between how many terms for color a language contained and the industrialization of the area where the language was spoken.

In other words, rather than finding that language controlled thought and perception, they found that culture was driving language, the opposite of the strong Sapir-Whorf conclusion.

If you look closely, the problems with the strong Sapir-Whorf hypothesis show through even in *Babel-17*.

While Rydra commands astonishing analytic super powers through her mastery of a variety of languages, she manages to explain her solutions to the people around her (and the reader) by using their common language. And she solves the psychological schism created by exposure to the language with no concept of "I" by introducing the concept. She calls her new creation Babel-18, versioning the original like a computer language, but what she's actually done is force the constructed language to behave like all other human languages by changing to meet the needs of its speakers.

The Weak, the Robust

While the strong version of the Sapir-Whorf hypothesis is fairly conclusively wrong, there is still plenty of room to explore the relationship between language, perception and thought.

Modern academia generally accepts the weak version of the hypothesis, the idea that language influences thought. This is obvious to anybody who has ever heard a radio commercial for French fries and consequently changed their lunch plans, but there's a wealth of experimental evidence to be found from investigations into priming and framing.

Priming is the phenomenon where exposure to a concept renders the subject likelier to return to the concept at a later time. For example, show a test subject a list of fifty multi-syllabic words. Then, several hours later, ask them to give you a word that begins with a syllable that is the first syllable of one of the words on the list. The test subject is highly likely to reply with the word from the list, even if they don't consciously remember having seen it. Language the test subject was exposed to earlier has influenced their later response without the test subject's awareness of the influence. (This also explains why sudden cravings for French fries are sometimes inexplicable.)

Framing is a phenomenon known in everyday life as "tact" or "spin-doctoring." It's the idea that how a situation is presented will change the audience's perception of the situation. Like priming, framing has a wealth of experimental data to support its existence. Framing experiments work like this:

Two groups of subjects are presented with a scenario where one thousand people are infected with a disease. The first group is given a choice between Treatment A, which will save three hundred people, or treatment B which has a 25% chance of saving all one thousand people and a 75% chance of saving nobody. The second group is given a choice between treatment A, which will allow seven hundred people to die, or treatment B which, again, has a 25% chance of saving all one thousand people and a 75% chance of saving nobody. Both groups have been given the exact same choice, but the first group has been presented with the positive frame while the second group has been given the negative frame. The first group is much more likely to choose treatment A, while the second group is much more likely to choose treatment B. The way language was used to present the situation changed how the subjects in either group evaluated the decision. Palafax of the Breakness Institute would be thrilled.

The Evolving Trope

While *Snow Crash* his hardly the only example of speculative work that engages with the genre tropes around language without updating them in light of modern research and understanding, there's a wealth of work which does better. The answer to Vance's devastating cultural division in *The Languages of Pao* comes exactly twenty years later in Ursula LeGuin's *The Dispossessed*.

Much like Palafax's plot, the Utopian society of Anarres creates its own language as part of its self-isolation from the society of Urras. But where the linguistic isolation becomes absolute and controlling in Vance's novel, LeGuin's spends a great deal of time exploring the ways in which the intended isolation fails, from a direct carryover of vocabulary such as "damn" and "hell" even though the new society doesn't have the concepts to which these words literally refer, to the way their informal social institutions wind up accidentally mimicking the structures of the society they've abandoned.

Stranger in a Strange Land's thesis about verbalizing species and concepts gets put to good work in C. J. Cherryh's 1994 *Foreigner*. The alien Atevi don't have words in their language for concepts like trust, friend, or love because they genuinely lack the concepts.

Bren, the human protagonist of the novel, struggles at length to communicate these concepts within the limits of the Atevi language by doing everything from positing hypothetical situations and pointing out the differences in predicted human and Atevi responses, to using Atevi words for concepts that are analogous in human languages. Bren's failure with the later tactic serves both as a fantastic illustration of how alien the Atevi are, and the differences between what you see when a concept is absent from language because the speakers have never gotten around to talking about it with each other, versus when it's absent because the speakers genuinely don't have it.

China Mieville's, *Embassytown* from 2011 delivers a similar treatment to the brain-hacking trope. There we are once again presented with aliens who are cognitively different from humans in a way that affects their language, the Ariekei. Unlike the humans or other sentient species in the novel, the Ariekei do operate in accordance with the strong version of the Sapir-Whorf hypothesis.

Mieville introduces this concept and then promptly allows the book to question whether the Ariekei are properly sentient. *Embassytown's* treatment of the brain-hacking trope doesn't rely on the flawed brain-as-computer analogy, providing instead a compelling exploration of how lies interact with a language that is, functionally, thought for its speakers.

So Here We Are

The strong version of the Sapir-Whorf hypothesis which enjoyed so much popularity in classic speculative fiction is wrong. However, that doesn't mean modern fiction must choose between using the tropes created by those early works and keeping in touch with modern research and understanding of language. The dialog between fiction, science, and genre history is ongoing, and there remains a wealth of ideas to be explored and examined. As our understanding of language and the human mind matures, the frontiers for our speculation will only grow more fascinating.

ABOUT THE AUTHOR

Anaea Lay lives in Madison, Wisconsin where she sells Real Estate under a different name, writes, cooks, plays board games, spoils her cat, runs the *Strange Horizons* podcast, and plots to take over the world. Her fiction has appeared in a variety of venues including *Apex, Lightspeed, Daily Science Fiction* and *Nightmare*.

Hard Truths in Our World: A Conversation with Bradley P. Beaulieu

JEREMY L. C. JONES

The world of Bradley P. Beaulieu's, The Lays of Anuskaya trilogy expands ever outward, with windships, mountain peaks, elemental spirits and archipelagos, greed and revenge—endlessly fascinating, always wondrous and evocative, even as the internal conflicts twist and swell and threaten to break even the strongest character.

Here is world-building at its best—character and setting intertwined, the interior and exterior landscapes equally compelling, and in constant interaction with each other.

It's hard to believe that the two entities—the world and the characters—haven't been created together, simultaneously.

"I really enjoy the character creation process," said Beaulieu, "but I'll be honest, I don't do much of it until I've completed the world-building to a fairly large degree."

Why? How? What good is a farmer without a farm? A seed without soil?

"The cultures and their histories are completely made up," said Beaulieu. "Yes, I borrow from Earth-based cultures, but I can't use them as-is, and I can't borrow from our own history at all. So all of that—the world and magic and cultures and histories—becomes the soil in which the story will grow."

By preparing the soil separately, Beaulieu ensures the interconnectedness as the characters grow.

"As I create more and more characters, I know where they came from, what biases they will have, what likes and dislikes will have been taught from a young age, and so on," he said. "And then they can become their own unique people, either subscribing to those biases or going against them. And that's when the tapestry of the story really starts to come alive, when the characters breathe life into it and play against not only one another, but the world in which they were born and raised."

Perhaps his method of building the world before the character—soil before planting, the nest before laying the egg—is not unique—but the result is certainly compelling. Beaulieu's novels achieve that rate effect of being richly textured, complex without being cluttered or garish.

To run wildly across a palette of metaphors—Beaulieu's prose is fine-grained, high resolution; it has a high thread count; and it's highly readable while rewarding careful attention to detail.

Furthermore, through all the violent disputes and irreconcilable differences, there is always a ray of hope. Below, Beaulieu and I talk about character and world-building, style and more.

How would you describe your style?

I would say I'm an amalgam of George R.R. Martin, C.S. Friedman, and Guy Gavriel Kay. I like Martin for his grittiness and the breadth and depth of his writing. The sheer amount of scope in his work is staggering, and I wanted to bring some of that sense of grand tapestry to my own work. Friedman I love for her serious and dark tone, the relentlessness of her storytelling, and the depth of her characters. It's a heady mix, particularly the Coldfire trilogy, which had a great effect on me and my writing. And Kay I love for his elegance of prose. His stories also tend to be romantic, and while I do like to bring a sense of grit to my stories, particularly when battle is at hand, I also think there's room for romanticism.

I picture my novels as rich pre-Raphaelite paintings, pulling in hues and tones from the writers who've had an effect on me. Or at least, that's how I would have described them as I was learning the ropes. Now I like to think that I'm moved beyond the point where I even notice my own style. It simply *is*, a part of me as much as what I choose to write about.

What do you enjoy about writing fiction, long or short?

I enjoy short fiction, but I *love* novel length work. There's something to be said, certainly, of the short form. I love it for its brevity, for the power it can pack in such a short space, for the wonderful flash of imagery it can give to the reader. But I grew up reading Tolkien, and then gravitating to things like Thomas Covenant the Unbeliever and The Belgariad and The Coldfire trilogy. The stories I loved most were the ones that had rich secondary worlds, the ones that had full cultures unlike our own, populated with magic and warriors and wizards. It's quite difficult to get the feel of those kind of worlds in a short story. Sure, you might catch a glimpse, but if you truly love a world, you want to spend more time in it.

And so it was with my writing. When I began toying with the idea, I did so with novels, but even when I started writing short fiction to stretch my writing muscles, I found myself creating entire secondary worlds in which to tell a 7,000-word tale. It was fun, but exhausting for so little output. Just as I want to explore and relate to characters I love while reading, I want to *inhabit* them while writing novels. I want to explore them more than short fiction will allow. Sure, I could write many short tales in a single world, but that means that the tale itself is but a glimpse of some larger tale. At least, it is for me. I tend to think in trilogies—an affliction so many of us, me included, can lay at the feet of Professor Tolkien—and so I want something large and grand to be told by the time I'm finally ready to put a story to rest.

What's at the heart of The Lays of Anuskaya trilogy? And did that change or drift or evolve at all over the years of writing the books?

The heart of The Lays of Anuskaya can be found in 9/11, the Iraq War, and the surrounding conflicts. Like so many people—not just Americans, but people all over the world—I was greatly affected by the events of 9/11. There was rage and confusion and a deep desire to "get to the bottom of it," to understand why the perpetrators of that crime had done what they'd done. The more I searched for answers, however, the more I realized that it's an endless story with endless causes and endless consequences.

I'm a pragmatist. There are hard truths in our world, and I understand the need for war in certain circumstances, but I'm also very much in the "can't we all just get along" camp. It was in that frustration that the seeds of the story were laid down, and they started to bear fruit as I fleshed out the conflict that's told in the story, one that has roots in the generations past but that's coming to a head just as the story opens.

The heart of the story—a tale of irreconcilable differences—didn't change very much in the telling. It continued to be the primary driver of what happened. But I was able to show where some people, if they try hard, can meet in the middle, and I was able to bring that new perspective to several different characters. That was one of the more gratifying things for me, to show a tale in which the characters learn and come to understand another culture from a perspective that was beforehand very limited. Not everyone ended up agreeing with the other side—that wouldn't be a truthful story—but they certainly *understood* more if nothing else, and all of that came from my inner desires for us, in this world, to do the same.

Where would you most like to visit in that world? Least like to visit?

I would have to say the island of Galahesh, where the Straits are. I wrote about this more in Mary Robinette Kowal's blog. It's a very interesting place because it stands between two worlds: the Empire of Yrstanla to the west and the islands of the Grand Duchy of Anuskaya to the east. It has parts of both, and so represents a lot of things in the world, and certainly for the second book, The Straits of Galahesh. I also like it from the sheer vista it would provide. I was struck when I visited the Cliffs of Moher near Galway, Ireland. It's a popular tourist attraction there, and you're able to go right up to the edge of the cliffs and stare straight down. I stayed there for over an hour and could have stayed for several more, just staring down at the churning sea below, the seagulls that were wheeling several hundred feet below my vantage point. It was amazing. And it would be incredible to see that in the form of the straits on Galahesh, with two tall cliffs and a massive bridge spanning them.

I think I'd least like to visit some of the islands to the east of the Grand Duchy. I was born and raised in Wisconsin, and I do enjoy a month or so of cold, but I would detest living like that for six or seven months out of the year. And it would be worse as barren as some of those islands are. Then again, with a warm fire and some vodka, perhaps it wouldn't be so bad...

Where did you start in building the world of the Anuskaya trilogy?

The origins of The Lays of Anuskaya was a bit multimedia in nature.

First, I used some artwork to help with inspiration. In 2004, my wife and I went to the National Gallery in Edinburgh, and we saw some wonderful paintings. I decided that my next project (which eventually became *The Winds of Khalakovo*) would include the artwork I bought in postcard form. At the time I was working on another novel. I was finishing up a draft and knew that it would need at least one more to make it work. I was also working heavily on short fiction. I went to Orson Scott Card's Literary Bootcamp the summer following, and Clarion the summer following that. Suffice it to say that the story didn't really get my full attention until around 2007, several years after spying the artwork. But that was great, actually, because I was still learning a lot about writing, which helped me to take on such a large project. Plus, the delay afforded my hindbrain to work on the story without the pressure of actually writing it. It was nice for the pressure to be off, so to speak, but of course the pressure was "on" in other pieces of fiction I was working on at the time.

Second, I used an excellent little piece of mapping software called Fractal Terrains. The program allows you to specify some basic parameters about a world—things like diameter, water coverage, mountain height and ocean depth, the number of moons—and the software will then render a world for you. I played with the software a lot, altering the parameters and retrying until I had something I liked. I knew that I wanted a world with archipelagos. The rendering of the terrain and the channels beneath the ocean surface ended up advising me on the magic of the world. It also created the geo-political structure. I circled the island chains until I had what I wanted: a loose collection of archipelagos that depended upon one another for survival. These became the Grand Duchy of Anuskaya, and two of my main characters became a Prince of one duchy and a Princess of another. It also made sense to me that there might have been an indigenous people on these islands that were pushed out by the expansion of the Grand Duchy. And from this flowed both the Aramahn, the peaceful peoples that originally inhabited the islands, and the Maharraht, the warlike splinter of the Aramahn that wish to push the Grand Duchy from the shores of the islands at any cost.

And how did you develop it from that original seed?

I mentioned earlier that I had some time to let it marinate, which was good for me. Perhaps even crucial to the success of the trilogy. It let the world mature, and the cultures, the histories between them, and so on, and that allowed more of the conflicts in the "current" story to manifest. Extra time also allows me to work on the magic systems, which I really want to be something unique and meaningful to the story and to be entwined with the history of the world. And that takes a lot of time. At least it does for me. I don't want the story to feel like it's a cheap veneer for a D&D spell manual, so I try to take care with the magic. I tend to use a light hand, á la J.R.R. Tolkien or George R.R. Martin, but even so, what lies beneath the page must be worked out in detail so that what's shown above the page makes sense and is internally consistent.

I really don't like diving too deeply into a story until I know a lot about the back story and magical elements of a world, so this developmental stage is a very important step for me. It's something I've continued to use since. I recently sold a new trilogy to DAW Books, a story about a pit fighter in a powerful desert city who rises to challenge the rule of the Twelve Kings. I had written a partial before selling the series, but before that I had worked on the world and characters and story for about two years. I'm doing the same for a middle grade series I'm working on now. And frankly, it's one of the most fun parts of writing for me, the creation of new worlds from scratch.

What are some of the cool things that got left out of the novels—places or ideas or scenes that didn't make it into the book?

I didn't really get a chance to explore many of the duchies in the Grand Duchy. The story had characters from all of the nine duchies, but I could only fit so many locales between the covers. It would have been fun to explore the other duchies more, to flesh out their shared history and their differences.

I also would have liked to explore the desert cultures that became more important to the story in the third book, *The Flames of Shadam Khoreh*. In Flames, the characters go to the great Gaji Desert to look for the fabled valley of Shadam Khoreh. I really do love Arabian Nights style tales, and I got to scratch that itch a bit in the writing of the third book. Then again, it was just the right amount for this particular story, and I do get to explore that milieu a lot in my next series, which will take place almost exclusively in a massive desert with sand-skimming sailing ships.

Where did you start *The Flames of Shadam Khoreh*—character, setting, idea, somewhere else all together? And how does that compare to the beginning point of the other novels in the trilogy?

The genesis of *The Flames of Shadam Khoreh* was in the rifts that are spreading throughout the world. We learn in *The Winds of Khalakovo* that these rifts exist. They are tears between the material world and the world of the spirits, which are elemental in nature: water, air, earth, fire, and life. These rifts were caused hundreds of years ago, but they're becoming worse—*much* worse as *The Flames of Shadam Khoreh* opens. I didn't know it when I first started writing *The Winds of Khalakovo*, but the rifts are the throughline for the entire series. The story in essence starts and must also end with them. It made for a satisfying story for me personally as the story in many ways came full circle from where it had begun. On the other hand, the world had changed greatly, and it was interesting seeing those two sides of the same coin play out.

In what ways did the writing of *The Flames of Shadam Khoreh* challenge you as a writer? What were some of the surprises it threw at you?

The biggest challenge for me was to pull in all the threads that I had set up in Book One and expanded on in Book Two. Those threads are unspoken promises to the reader. They have a certain trajectory and they create within the reader certain expectations: not only that they will be resolved, but resolved in a satisfying way. And that "satisfying" formula is a very difficult one to solve. You want to create surprise in the reader without surprising them *too* much. You want conflict without it becoming overly chaotic. You want change in character without it being either predictable or illogical. There are so many things to get right, and the ending of a story, especially for something so broad as an epic fantasy, it's a tricky thing to do. Well, who am I kidding? It's tricky in *any* genre. And it certainly was in this case. I was very pleased with how it turned out, and I hope the fans of the series are too.

What's next for you?

I mentioned the two series I'm working on above. One is called *The Song of the Shattered Sands* and will be coming out from DAW Books in 2014. Here's the blurb for the first book in the series, Twelve Kings in Sharakhai:

In the cramped west end of Sharakhai, the Amber Jewel of the Desert, Çeda fights in the pits to scrape a living. She, like so many in the city, pray for the downfall of the cruel, immortal Kings of Sharakhai, but she's never been able to do anything about it. This all changes when she goes out on the night of Beht Zha'ir, the holy night when all are forbidden from walking the streets. It's the night that the asirim, the powerful yet wretched creatures that protect the Kings from all who would stand against them, wander the city and take tribute. It is then that one of the asirim, a pitiful creature who wears a golden crown, stops Çeda and whispers long forgotten words into her ear. Çeda has heard those words before, in a book left to her by her mother, and it is through that one peculiar link that she begins to find hidden riddles left by her mother. As Çeda begins to unlock the mysteries of that fateful night, she realizes that the very origin of the asirim and the dark bargain the Kings made with the gods of the desert to secure them may be the very key she needs to throw off the iron grip the Kings have had over Sharakhai. And yet the Kings are no fools—they've ruled the Shangazi for four hundred years for good reason, and they have not been idle. As Çeda digs into their past, and the Kings come closer and closer to unmasking her, Çeda must decide if she's ready to face them once and for all. The other project I've just started writing is a middle grade series called *The Tales of the Bryndlholt*. It's set in a secondary world, but it will be loosely based off of our own Norse mythology. The story itself is about a group of misfit kids who usher in the end of the world.

Any parting words?

Only a quick thank you for having me by, and a shout-out for fans of science fiction and fantasy to check out the podcast I run with fellow author and English professor Gregory A. Wilson. The show is called Speculate! The Podcast for Writers, Readers, and Fans, and on it we talk about the field of speculative fiction, review works both short and long, discuss writing technique, and interview authors. We've had the pleasure of having on our show authors like Robin Hobb, Patrick Rothfuss, James Patrick Kelly, Brent Weeks, Kij Johnson, and many more.

ABOUT THE AUTHOR _____

Jeremy L. C. Jones is a freelance writer, editor, and teacher. He is the Staff Interviewer for *Clarkesworld Magazine* and a frequent contributor to *Kobold Quarterly* and *Booklifenow.com*. He teaches at Wofford College and Montessori Academy in Spartanburg, SC. He is also the director of Shared Worlds, a creative writing and world-building camp for teenagers that he and Jeff VanderMeer designed in 2006. Jones lives in Upstate South Carolina with his wife, daughter, and flying poodle.

Another Word: What I Did on My Summer Vacation
JAMIE TODD RUBIN

Summer vacations often encapsulate our fondest memories and this year was no exception. I had the privilege of spending seven days of my summer at the University of Wyoming, Laramie, eating dorm food, sleeping in dorm beds, and walking a few miles each day to get to the various classrooms on campus. Oh, and for about twelve hours each day, I sat in lectures on everything from phases of the moon to the spectral analysis of stars to black holes and the very foundations of the universe itself. I did all of this with a dozen other classmates, all of them writers trying to get a better understanding of astronomy and how to communicate it through their writing.

This was the Launch Pad Astronomy workshop, and I'm not sure I could have dreamed up a better summer vacation if I tried.

What is Launch Pad?

As the website describes it: "Launch Pad is a workshop for established writers in beautiful high-altitude Laramie, Wyoming. Launch Pad aims to provide a 'crash-course' for the attendees in modern astronomy science through guest lectures, and observations through the University of Wyoming's professional telescopes."

Actually, Launch Pad turned out to be a whole lot more. We had amazing lectures, some of them given by Mike Brotherton, a science fiction writer himself, and a professional astronomer at the University. Other talks were given by Andria Schwortz, a graduate student at the University and a science fiction fan and gamer in her own right. Our guest lecturer this year was Christian Ready, who has worked on the Hubble Telescope, and who has had his nonfiction about Hubble published in *Analog.*

Beyond the lectures, however, was a camaraderie that can only be conjured from a mixture of intensive study, eating all of your meals together, hanging out in the bar until the wee hours of the night, and talking shop in the lounge on your breaks.

We sat through hours of fascinating lectures and we bonded with an easy camaraderie. The result was a group of people who came out of seven days exhausted, but with a much better understanding of basic astronomy, as well as an appreciation for the art of telling stories and communicating what we learned in a meaningful way.

During our week at Launch Pad, our unofficial motto became, "Not To Scale," and that phrase describes Launch Pad very well. Launch Pad is not to scale. It is much, much bigger than it seems.

Dramatis Personae

This year marked Launch Pad's seventh year of operation. Launch Pad selects a diverse group of attendees for each of its classes and our group was no exception.

Our group included: Liz Argall, Chaz Brenchley, Jenn Brissett, Jennifer Campbell-Hicks, Brenda Clough, Douglas Dechow, Doug Farren, Claudine Griggs, Caren Gussoff, Anna Leahy, Jay O'Connell, Andrew Penn Romine, Jeri Smith-Ready, and, of course, me.

Several people—Andy, Liz, and Caren—were all alumni of Clarion and so they had previous experience in intensive, writing-related workshops. This was a first for me, and initially, I was amazed at how quickly we all bonded.

Looking back on it, I should not have been so surprised. Like the stars we studied, we all burn with the same essential elements: the desire to create, the desire to write, and the desire to learn more about the universe that we live in.

Learning fuels the desire, the desire drives the creativity. We all have that, and because of that, it seemed to me that we all found ourselves on the same wavelength.

A few of us—Chaz, Doug Farren and I—were early risers and would walk over to the student union at 7 am to squeeze in a few hours of writing before lectures started. Sometimes, Brenda would join us there.

At 8:30 each morning, the vast majority of us would head over to the Turtle Rock Cafe and have breakfast together. We'd take up half the restaurant, eating our bagels or egg scrambles and talking shop, or talking about things completely unrelated to writing, depending upon the moods of the moment.

Hands-On Science

We had three or four (and sometimes more) lectures each day. To reinforce what we learned, we had practical, hands-on activities. These experiences took us out of the classroom and gave us a feel for what it was like to work as a professional astronomer.

On the evening of our second day at Launch Pad, we headed up to the roof of the physical sciences building where three small telescopes had been prepared for our use. The moon had just passed its first quarter, and even so, once the sun set, the sky was filled with stars.

For attendees who live in big metropolitan areas, it was a wonderful sight. We saw Saturn with its rings and Titan lingering at a distance to one side. We looked at the terminator on the moon. We looked at binary star systems.

At one point during the evening, Mike Brotherton brought out his night-vision goggles. Looking at the night sky through them is a breathtaking experience. Instead of the few thousand stars you typically see, you can see *millions*. Occasionally I'd hear a hiss of breath sucked in from somewhere nearby and know that someone was looking through those glasses.

Later that evening, we were able to see the Andromeda galaxy. Seeing it was amazing and it gave perhaps the truest sense of scale and proportion. The Andromeda galaxy is some two *million* light years distant, and looking at the blurred object through those goggles, we were looking two million years back in time.

On another evening, we headed up to the Wyoming Infrared Observatory (WIRO) some ten thousand feet above sea-level and got to watch undergraduates in astronomy at work, this time using a 2.3-meter infrared telescope.

There were also other, smaller activities. In one instance, we learned to identify elements by their spectra. In another lab, we took raw images taken from Hubble and other telescopes in different frequencies of light, and learned to put them together and clean up the noise in the image.

We also learned how to look at the light curve of stars. We attempted to find the telltale drop-off in light that might indicate the transit of a planet. It is even possible that a member of the class, Douglas Dechow, discovered a planet surrounding a distant star as the drop-off on one of his stars was both regular and strong!

Getting our hands dirty in the real science that makes astronomy so fascinating was a crucial part of Launch Pad. Writers are often told "Write what you know," and most of us, especially science fiction writers, tend to eschew that advice. None of us have ever visited distant worlds, or orbited black holes. But learning how to take raw images and create works of art with them; or looking through night vision goggles and seeing Andromeda, these are things we have done and they reinforce our imaginations.

My Launch Pad Takeaways

Launch Pad is not just for people who write hard science fiction stories. Indeed, it is for anyone who writes science fiction, or science non-fiction for that matter. It is an equally wonderful experience for amateur astronomers.

Part of what I took from Launch Pad was an intensive refresher on basic astronomy. I learned why it would be silly to have a character's blood boil away if they were exposed to space. I learned subtleties of world-building, like how the axial tilt of a planet affects the seasons of that world. And I learned why we would be unlikely to find planets with intelligent life around class A stars. These takeaways improve the science in my stories.

I also made fifteen new friends at Launch Pad. Most of them are writers. We have many other friends in common, but now, we also have the week we spent at Launch Pad together, sitting in lectures, eating our meals, talking about movies, baseball or our favorite authors and stories.

I came away from Launch Pad with half a dozen story ideas based on the things we learned there, but I also came away with a solid foundation of basic astronomy, a must-have for a science fiction writer.

I was six years old when I got my first telescope, and throughout this workshop, I kept wishing that I could go back in time and tell my younger self, "Kid, you think this is cool? Just wait. Just wait . . . "

ABOUT THE AUTHOR ─────────────────────────

Jamie Todd Rubin is a science fiction writer, blogger, and Evernote Ambassador for paperless lifestyle. His stories and articles have appeared in *Analog, Daily Science Fiction, Lightspeed, Intergalactic Medicine Show, Apex Magazine,* and 40K Books. Jamie lives in Falls Church, Virginia with his wife and two children. Find him on Twitter at @jamietr.

Editor's Desk:
Year Seven by the Numbers
NEIL CLARKE

In June 2012, I wrote an editorial for the data junkies and people who wanted to get a snapshot of the data we have about *Clarkesworld*. Since then, I've received numerous requests to reprise the research as an annual "year in review." As we've just finished up our seventh year of publication, I thought this would be a good time to look back at that year. Unless otherwise specified, all of the information below is based on data collected between October 2012 and September 2013.

Where the Stories Come From

Unlike our early days, the majority of the stories we publish are un-solicited and submitted to us via an online form. This is commonly referred to as the slush pile. In year seven, we received 9241 stories and of those, we purchased thirty-two, an acceptance rate of 0.35%. On average, authors received a response from us in less than three days.

Despite the slush pile favoring men 71% to 29%, 65% of the purchased stories were written by women. In our seventh year, we published thirty-six stories—some were purchased outside this window or solicited directly from an author—and 68% of those were written by women.

We've always been off the norm for science fiction magazines, but last time the balance shifted like this, we took some flack. You have to keep in mind that slush pile data is quantitative, so it doesn't cleanly map to a qualitative process like selecting stories for publication. This data suggests that women were better at sending us the type of stories we were looking for this year.

YEAR	MEN	WOMEN	% WOMEN
2006-2007	10	14	58.3%
2007-2008	13	12	48.0%
2008-2009	12	13	52.0%
2009-2010	13	11	45.8%
2010-2011	8	16	66.7%
2011-2012	16	18	52.9%
2012-2013	11.5	24.5	68.1%
TOTAL	**83.5**	**108.5**	**56.5**

Gender of authors publishing stories in *Clarkesworld* by year.

One thing I noticed was that about half of our female contributors had sold stories to us before and most of the male authors were new to *Clarkesworld*. While it would be nice if our male regulars were more active, overall I can't complain about the quality of the stories we are receiving.

This year, we bought:

22 - Science Fiction stories (of 3619 submitted)
5 - Science Fiction + Fantasy stories (of 698 submitted)
3 - Fantasy + Horror stories (of 893 submitted)
3 - Fantasy stories (of 2464 submitted)
1 - "Other" stories (of 274 submitted)
0 - Horror stories (of 836 submitted)
0 - Science Fiction + Horror stories (of 457 submitted)

Note: Genre identification was done by the author at the time of submission. I'm not going to get into the "what is real SF?" fight.

Overall, men were more likely to write science fiction, women were more likely to write fantasy and horror was extremely male-dominated. There wasn't anything unusual when compared to other years.
Some other miscellaneous slush pile nuggets:

• Men favor submitting stories on Monday/Tuesday
• Women favor Tuesday/Wednesday
• Saturday is everyone's least favorite day to submit a story
• We received 929 submissions in August 2013 (new record)
• We rejected 920 submissions in July 2013 (new record)

Social Media

Most of our marketing efforts are centered on social media. At the moment we have 6603 likes on our Facebook Page and 9872 followers on Twitter. While Twitter doesn't share data with us, Facebook does provide some demographic information about the people that like our page:

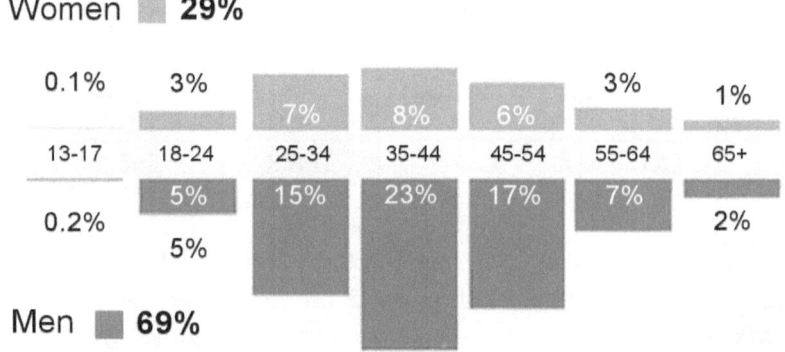

Women ■ 29%

0.1%	3%	7%	8%	6%	3%	1%
13-17	18-24	25-34	35-44	45-54	55-64	65+
0.2%	5%	5%	15%	23%	17%	7%	2%

Men ■ 69%

In June 2012, we had 3500 likes and women made up 33.5% of that population. We've picked up more than 3000 new likes in the last year and it appears that our male Facebook audience is growing faster than our female Facebook audience. Facebook claims that 55% of their users are male, so that doesn't seem unreasonable. The current numbers line up nicely with our submissions data as well.

As you can see in the above chart, the majority of Facebook audience falls between the ages of 25 and 54, with the largest concentration between 35 and 44. Overall, there doesn't appear to be a connection between gender and age. Given that Facebook's largest community of users are between the ages of 18 and 24, it would appear that we aren't connecting as well with that group. Without further research, we have no way of determining whether or not this indicates a lack of interest on their part or a marketing problem on ours. It is certainly worth looking into.

Around the World

One of the advantages of publishing a digital magazine is international distribution. People from all over the world read or listen to our stories, but where are they? Facebook claims our top five countries are: USA, UK, Canada, Australia, and Ireland. Our website statistics indicate that our web-based readers are from USA, UK, Canada, Australia, Germany, China and 191 other countries, 9% of which use browsers with languages set to something other than English. Libsyn, the service that hosts our podcast files, claims that our top five countries USA, UK, Canada, Australia, and China. The big surprise in this year's data was discovering Iran in sixth place among podcast downloads.

Reading

According to a very conservative interpretation of our web statistics, *Clarkesworld* has an average online readership of approximately thirty-three thousand.

Our podcast has between six and seven thousand listeners per month and each story picks up at least another two-to-three thousand listeners over the next eleven months.

Two thousand seven hundred readers are paid subscribers to our ebook editions at Weightless Books and Amazon. Our iPad, iPhone and Android apps just launched in October, so they'll count into next year's data.

All of these groups are likely to have some overlap with one another, so I use the thirty-three thousand number as the safe estimate of our overall readership. Some other quick facts about our readers and their habits are:

- December is the month with the lowest average daily readership.
- September was the highest.
- 60% of the visitors to our website are using Windows, 20% Mac, 11% IOS, and 7% Android.
- Chrome is the browser of choice for most of you, taking a 35% share with Firefox (24%), Safari (19%), and IE (10%) following behind.
- For podcasts—iTunes dominates with over 50%. Nothing else is even close to competing.

Business Data

- Only about 8% of our readers have paid subscriptions.
- 0.5% donate any amount.

Despite those low numbers, these are the people that keep *Clarkesworld* afloat. Our other revenue streams—advertising, the annual anthologies, print issues, etc.—contribute to the bottom line, but in-total, they only covered the expense of a single issue.

I've mentioned a few of our goals in past editorials. This is what it would take to accomplish them:

- To add that long-awaited fourth story in each issue, we need to convince another 1% of our online readership to subscribe.
- When 15% of our current readers have subscribed, our staff pay will reach the level where *Clarkesworld* will become my full-time job.

I don't doubt that some people will try to use these numbers to demonstrate how awful giving away free content is for business, but that ignores the inherent marketing value it provides to *Clarkesworld* and our authors. I won't pretend that it isn't just the tiniest bit frustrating, but it isn't unexpected and I continue to have faith in this business model.

So that's a quick look at the numbers for last year. If people are interested in getting more details or discussing what I've shared, I'd be happy to have that discussion in the comments area on our website. Next month, I plan to continue talking about what it takes to produce an issue of *Clarkesworld*. Numbers alone will never give you the whole picture.

ABOUT THE AUTHOR

Neil Clarke is the editor of *Clarkesworld Magazine*, owner of Wyrm Publishing and a 2013 Hugo Nominee for Best Editor (short form). He currently lives in NJ with his wife and two children.

About the Artist
PIOTR FOKSOWICZ

Piotr Foksowicz (piofoks) is a digital painter and concept artist from Poland. Piotr's work often incorporates fantasy and post-apocalyptic elements and his professional credits include many pieces for card games and book covers.

WEBSITE

piofoks.deviantart.com